THE IRE OF IRON CLAW

GADGETS AND GEARS

THE IRE OF IRON CLAW

2

Kersten Hamilton

with illustrations by

James Hamilton

HOUGHTON MIFFLIN HARCOURT

Boston   New York

For information about permission to reproduce selections from this
book, write to trade.permissions@hmhco.com or to Permissions,
Houghton Mifflin Harcourt Publishing Company,
3 Park Avenue, 19th Floor, New York, New York 10016.

www.hmhco.com

The text of this book is set in Plantin.
The illustrations were executed digitally.
Design by Sharismar Rodriguez

The Library of Congress has cataloged the hardcover edition as follows:
Hamilton, K. R. (Kersten R.)
The ire of Iron Claw / Kersten Hamilton ; with illustrations by James
Hamilton.
pages cm — (Gadgets and gears ; book 2)
Summary: "The daring and loyal dachshund Noodles, the boy inventor
Wally Kennewickett, and his scientific genius family and staff of automatons
join forces with Nikola Tesla to defeat sky pirates, cross Europe in a giant
mechanical spider, and defy the evil Mesmers"—Provided by publisher.
[1. Adventure and adventurers—Fiction. 2. Dachshunds—Fiction.
3. Dogs—Fiction. 4. Hypnotism—Fiction. 5. Inventions—Fiction. 6.
Robots—Fiction. 7. Pigeons—Fiction. 8. Tesla, Nikola, 1856–1943—Fiction.
9. Humorous stories. 10. Science fiction.] I. Hamilton, James
(James Clayson), 1981– illustrator. II. Title.
PZ7.H1824Ire 2015
[Fic]—dc23
2014027742

ISBN: 978-0-544-22502-2 hardcover
ISBN: 978-0-544-66854-6 paperback

Manufactured in the United States of America
DOC 10 9 8 7 6 5 4 3 2 1
4500589590

This book is for Charlie.

—K.H.

If you reside along the rails, you may have heard of a boy named Wally and his best friend, the flying dachshund. You may have heard rumors that this daring duo saved a train full of passengers from plummeting to their deaths. The rumors are true.

My name is Noodles. I am that dachshund.

More had rested upon the brilliant boy's shoulders than even the rail men guessed. Walter Kennewickett, scientist in training, had not only invented the wings that saved the train, but also stymied Madini the magician and the peculiar pigeon Iron Claw in their attempt to capture President Theodore Roosevelt and subvert his will.

"Subvert" is a very unpleasant word. It means to overthrow completely.

Madini was apparently the mastermind of an evil organization that called itself the Mesmers. As everyone knows, the first and most famous rule of evil organizations is: *Try to take over the world.* The second and only slightly less famous edict of evildoers happens to be: *When foiled, seek vengeance.*

"Vengeance" is a *particularly* unpleasant word. In the weeks since Iron Claw and Madini had appeared at the Kennewicketts' Automated Inn, I had become acutely aware of many unpleasant words, including *subvert, sabotage,* and *mind transference.* When the Mesmers sought vengeance, I felt it would be against the fearless boy who had foiled their plans. But by far the most unsettling word I had overheard in recent weeks—more unsettling even than vengeance—was the word *mole.*

You might think a mole is a small brown creature that lives in the dark and eats worms.

But there is another kind of mole: a person you know and trust who is betraying you.

Calypso, Wally's mother, believed that there must be a mole at the Automated Inn. Oliver, Wally's father, could not believe any of the Kennewicketts' friends or family capable of such subterfuge.

But neither could he explain how top-secret research papers had disappeared from his seemingly secure lab, subsequently to be published in Italy as the works of one Signore Giuseppe, a man famous not for science but for his copious coops of racing pigeons.

Both Oliver and Calypso agreed that the amazing automaton Gizmo should add one more job to her already busy schedule. In addition to scientific assistant and head cook, they had appointed her chief of security of the Automated Inn. Being an automaton, Gizmo was immune to the Mesmers' mind control. Being Gizmo, she had the architect's original drawings of the Inn stored in her mechanical mind. She was familiar with every nook and cranny where a mole might try to conceal himself.

Gizmo's tireless toil left the Kennewicketts free to attend to other business. On this particular morning, that business was our Annual Open House.

I had been flitting about the crowds all morning, wearing the wonderful wings Wally had designed for me. I searched the skies above for pigeons—and the crowds below for somnambulists, mustachioed Mesmers, or bizarre behavior that might betray a mole. My tail was tired, and an undeniable emptiness was gnawing at my middle. Wagging to keep myself aloft was a great deal of work, and it had been hours since I'd eaten breakfast, but I dared not rest.

I'd appointed myself Wally Kennewickett's *personal* security force. I had failed once, when I had not detected the scent of approaching danger. I would not fail Wally again. Everyone from the townspeople to the hobos who camped by the river had been invited to the Open House. I had a lot of patrolling to do.

"Hello, Noodles," Mayor McDivit called from the deck of the *Daedalus* as I flew past. Oliver and Calypso were conducting tours of the aerostat extraordinaire, a lighter-than-air craft designed to resemble a sailing vessel.

The citizens of Gasket Gully fled in fright the first time the *Daedalus* weighed anchor over Irma's Ice Cream Parlor so that Wally could descend by rope ladder to buy a treat. They had mistaken her for the *Flying Dutchman,* a ghost ship that sails the sky as a harbinger of doom.

Oliver appeared on deck, bullhorn in hand, to explain that what appeared to be masts,

bowsprit, and spars were actually vanes for recording wind direction, electrometers for detecting atmospheric electrons, and various versions of lightning rods.

I tipped my wings to the mayor and dove lawnward, where Prissy Kennewickett, Wally's almost-grown-up cousin, was performing a one-woman circus show. A stray ball from the lawn tennis tournament that her twin, Melvin, was officiating arced toward me. I caught it in midair and returned it to the court before rising into the sky again.

Everything seemed peaceful.

But no matter how hard I shook my ears, I could not dislodge the feeling that had settled over me as the sun rose that morning. *Something horrible was about to happen.* Such a feeling of dread can keep even a hungry dachshund aloft.

"Noo-dles!" Wally's call drifted to me on the wind. "I need you!" I wheeled, wagging wildly, my every whisker alert as I rose above the parapet that crowns the Inn. There were neither Mesmers nor moles in sight. At the far end of the roof stood the original stone turret, topped by Oliver's Gyrating Generator and accessible only by scaling a wind-swept ladder. A mysterious new tower had risen beside it.

Closer at hand, a cluster of townspeople were watching the boy scientist. Walter Kennewickett's contribution to the delights of the day was a demonstration of his clever man-lifting kite. Today, however, it would be a watermelon-lifting kite instead. Calypso was not yet convinced of the contraption's safety.

Wally had designed the kite in order to test the principles of wing angle as described by Mr. Wilbur Wright, a bicycle builder and aeronautical experimenter. Wally was adjusting the altitude of the rail cannon, the device that would launch his invention into the air.

I realized the problem at once, of course. The folded kite, with its cleverly concealed deployment device, which should have been affixed to the back of the chair that sat on said retractable rail cannon, was missing.

"Noodles," Wally said as I settled on the

rooftop beside him, "could you find Gizmo for me? She hasn't delivered the kite, and I'm sure I shouldn't leave our guests!"

I barked agreement and prepared to make my way through the gathered gawkers to the belvedere.

A "belvedere" is a building or room set on a high spot and situated in such a way as to command an excellent view.

Our spacious rooftop belvedere was completely enclosed due to the constant winds. Three walls were of stone, but the fourth was constructed of glass. The guests gathered around Wally had no doubt taken the time to look out over their town and the valley beyond before they'd stepped through the door in one of the stone walls and onto the roof. There were several more huddled around that doorway now, most of them awed by the expanse of blue sky above.

I saw a few familiar faces among them.

Theoden McDivit, Mayor McDivit's son and Wally's second-best friend, had brought his camera to document the day. Old Mrs. Dory

McDivit, Theoden's great-grandmother, was there to watch over him.

Mr. Jones, the engineer, train driver, cookie chef, and collector of conspiracy theories, was standing beside her.

Mr. Jones had been of great service to the Kennewicketts during the incident with Iron Claw. It was his train that we had saved. Even now, his Iron Road Irregulars, fashioned after the information-gathering organization of Mr. Doyle's fictional detective Sherlock Holmes, were collecting clues along the railways of America. Mr. Jones claimed his Irregulars were more ubiquitous than Mr. Roosevelt's Secret Service. By that he meant that they were everywhere. They must have been invisible as well, because I had never seen them.

Mr. Jones was very fond of Dory McDivit. I could not imagine why. She smelled of pickled beets, slipped extra pastries in her purse whenever she came to dinner, and sometimes said terrible things about Wally. But I was certain she was neither a Mesmer nor a mole.

Before I reached the belvedere, Gizmo and Jeeves, the mechanical butler, appeared in its doorway, bearing the bundled kite.

"The folding device needed oil," Gizmo apologized, "and had to be shut off for a moment."

"I am sure you did your best," Wally said. "Noodles can attend to the guests while we finish here."

I wagged, eager to help Wally, even though I was uncertain of how much longer my wag might last. I raced in circles, then leaped into the air and executed a loop-the-loop. Mr. Jones led the citizens in a rousing round of huzzahs.

"Why are they cheering?" Mrs. McDivit demanded, turning her ear trumpet toward her great-grandson. "Don't they know bats are dangerous?"

Theoden pulled his head from beneath the canvas hood of his camera and shouted into the trumpet. "It's not a bat, Grandmamma. It's a dachshund. One more loop, Noodles!" he called. "I want to capture you on camera!"

I wasn't sure I had the energy. My wagger

was starting to wilt. In fact, I was beginning to sink when Mr. Jones pulled a snickerdoodle from his pocket and tossed it into the air.

"Mad Mars kept bats," Mrs. McDivit bellowed as I swooped for the sweet. "I used to throw rocks at them!"

I caught the cookie in midflight. Strengthened, I hovered before Theoden's lens.

"Bats carry hydrophoby," Mrs. McDivit declared. "It's deadly!"

She meant "hydrophobia," of course, known in canines as "rabics." Well-bred dachshunds do *not* get rabies.

"All set, Noodles!" Wally called.

Apparently unaware of my excellent breeding, several citizens of Gasket Gully backed away from me as I settled on the rooftop.

"Never mind, Noodles," Mr. Jones said, scooping me up. "Dory means well. But she knew old Mars, you see."

"I'll want a photo before you pull the lever, Wally," Theoden said. Theoden planned to sell photographs of Wally's inventions to Ogden's

Collectible Trading Cards. Theoden and Wally have two hundred and fifty-four of the trading cards between them.

Most recently Wally had traded three cards—a Quadrant Motorcycle with a Minerva Clip-On Engine, a Croudus Electric Carriage, and a Locomobile Steam Automobile—to Theoden for a single coveted card: the eight-legged land-and-air yacht *Arachne*, created by Monsieur Fevre of France.

Arachne was a very rare card. I could not imagine why. Watching a spider crawl across the floor always gave me the shivers, and their method of aerial transport is worse. Perhaps you have observed an arachnid performing this unnatural act? It leans

forward as if kissing the ground, tips its abdomen up, and emits a silken parachute, which carries it into the sky.

There is nothing so unsettling as coming face-to-face with a spider a thousand feet above the ground.

Wally had been encouraged to correspond with Monsieur Fevre by Theodore Roosevelt himself. Our president not only had a keen interest in science; he also had friends and admirers all over the world. Happily, the *Arachne*'s inventor still resided in the country of his birth. Wally wasn't likely to inveigle a visit to the mechanical monstrosity.

To "inveigle" means to entice or coax.

"Wait," Wally said, glancing at the wind gauge. "It's gusting!"

"Disgusting!" Mrs. McDivit shouted. "I quite agree!"

Another loop, eh, Noodles?" Mr. Jones suggested, setting me down and slipping a second snickerdoodle from his pocket.

I was in the air instantly. I am easily inveigled when snickerdoodles are involved. I caught the cookie at the top of my loop, and was licking my whiskers when I landed.

"The winds have shifted to the right direction," Wally announced. "We are ready to launch!"

"Wait!" Theoden said as Wally gripped the lever. "Hold it right there, everyone!" I had to admit it was a terrific tableau.

A "tableau" is a picturesque arrangement of people or objects.

Wally looked dashing in his lab coat and

goggles. His long, striped scarf flapped smartly in the wind. His copper-colored hair was unruly, as it always was when he was inventing. Gizmo was standing beside the boy scientist, looking cunning in her cap and clockwork corset. The small twitch she had recently developed was hardly noticeable. Gizmo was overdue for an upgrade.

Mr. Jones pressed his hand to his heart and sighed when she smiled for the camera. The engineer's ardent admiration for the workings of her mechanical mind had recently developed into something more. He had given her his snickerdoodle recipe.

Jeeves, the oversize butler who stood behind Gizmo, was not quite so sightly. In fact, his grim visage could be considered frightening. His iron grip held a bumbershoot aloft, defying the wind in order to give Wally shade as he readied the cannon.

I comforted myself with the thought that Dory McDivit could not possibly know that the butler standing before her had once attempted

to use that very cannon to bombard the town of Gasket Gully in a bid to take over the world. An electrical surge had eventually melted Jeeves's wiring, ending his erratic behavior. The aberrant automaton had been dismantled immediately, of course.

In defense of the Kennewicketts' creations, it was highly unusual for an automaton to attempt world domination.

Nonetheless, Calypso had reengineered the remaining members of the electronic staff so that they could neither detain nor deter a Kennewickett. Their wiring would ignite if they even attempted it.

Oliver had recently revisited the pile of parts that was Jeeves, recalibrating every gear in his cranium before reattaching the head. Oliver Kennewickett believes in second chances. (It is rumored that Calypso gave Oliver himself a second chance after some scientific shenanigans while they were wooing. That was before my time, of course.)

Jeeves himself had no record of the events

that caused him to be dismantled—his mechanical memory had melted away, along with his wiring.

Calypso's reengineering meant that the mole we were seeking could not be an automaton.

"Got the shot," Theoden said. "Let her go up!"

"Blow up?" Mrs. McDivit screeched, taking a step back. "What is he going to blow up?"

"Nothing, Dory," Mr. Jones boomed into her ear trumpet. "Walter is launching a kite."

"Nonsense," the lady said. "That boy's the spit and image of Mad Mars himself. Mark my words—something is going to blow up. It always does with the Kennewicketts."

Wally pulled the lever. The chair left the rails, rocketing skyward as a steel line unspooled behind it. When it reached the extent of the steel cable, five hundred feet above us, the resulting tug triggered a tiny explosive charge. The pack popped like a party cracker.

The kite bloomed, and the watermelon hung triumphant in the sky.

"I'd like to try that ride myself," Mr. Jones said. "Imagine the view!"

I didn't have to imagine it. I'd seen it: the rooftop with its Gyrating Generator, atmospheric instruments, and the tremendous new copper-topped tower that had recently been completed; the lawn with its miniature circus on one side and Melvin's lawn-tennis nets on the other. Then, in the valley below, the town of Gasket Gully, and beyond it the mighty waters of the Oblivion River rushing out of the mountains.

"Excellent launch, young sir!" Jeeves said, adjusting the bumbershoot to give Wally more shade.

"Shall I reel it in now?" Gizmo asked.

"Please do," Wally replied, removing his gloves in order to scratch my ears. "And would you be so kind as to see the kite refolded before you check on the kitchen? We'll launch again as soon as possible. I don't know how long the winds will be in our favor."

The wind is always blowing at the Inn. But at the colossal kite's extreme altitudes, the winds could be incredibly strong. If the Inn had not been built of stone and rooted in the mountain itself, I would have feared it might be pulled from its foundation by Wally's contraption.

"Of course," Gizmo said.

"One more picture, Wally," Theoden requested. "You and Noodles together!"

"Wal-ter!" Prissy called up from below, just as the camera's flash spat sparks above Theoden. I raced to the parapet and looked over it, Wally by my side.

Prissy was swinging by her knees on her high trapeze. At the apogee of her arc, she released the bar and did a somersault in the air before landing lightly on the platform. An "apogee" is the farthest or highest point of something.

"Calypso would like us to bring our guests to brunch," Prissy said when she could make herself heard over the applause of the crowd gathered on the lawn beneath her. "And summon the Wizard while you are at it!"

She was referring to the Kennewicketts' friend Mr. Nikola Tesla, the architect of the mysterious copper-topped tower I previously mentioned.

Prissy had just finished a book by Mr. L. Frank Baum in which there was a wizard in a wonderful land called Oz. She was much taken by the fact that Mr. Tesla was frequently referred to as "the Wizard of the West" in newsprint accounts of his accomplishments.

I didn't find it at all applicable. Mr. Baum's wizard was a faker and a fraud. Mr. Tesla was a man with a mind so keen his electrical inventions seemed like magic, not only to the public but to other scientists as well. The Mesmers had spoiled a very important experiment that Oliver and Mr. Tesla had been working on, and he had hurried to the Inn to find out what went wrong.

Mr. Tesla had been very concerned when he learned of Iron Claw. He was a lover of pigeons, and well-known for feeding them in the park.

Two weeks after the brilliant scientist's arrival, construction on the mysterious tower had begun. Only Oliver, Calypso, and the Wizard himself knew what its function was.

"We'll be right down!" Wally called.

"Shall I summon Mr. Tesla to brunch for you, young sir?" Jeeves asked.

"No, thank you, Jeeves," Wally said. "I'll do it. You'll be needed in the dining room, and I need to tidy myself before appearing there."

I agreed. Wally's mother believes that a well-kempt appearance is a sign of a well-kempt mind. She would never condone wearing a lab coat to brunch.

"As Mr. Tesla's room is next to my own," Wally went on, "it will cause no delay."

"Very good, sir," Jeeves said with a bow.

Wally turned the guests over to Gizmo, and I raced to reach the door as soon as it was open. I was eager for brunch, but that was not the only reason I moved so fast.

3

You may recall from my previous adventure that Dust Bunnies are small, annoying automatons. It is their job to clean the Automated Inn. It is *my* job to keep them out of sight when we have guests. I find them by far the most troublesome of Calypso's creations. Dust Bunnies don't depend on electrons, like their more elegant cousins. They have springs and keys and must be wound, and they insist on popping up everywhere they shouldn't be—for instance, in the belvedere, which is always as neat as a pin. The marble floor is polished, the west windows gleam, and there are never crumbs on the tiny tables or comfortable chairs scattered throughout the room. Even the stairs leading down to the Inn rarely need dusting.

I wriggled through the door as soon as it was open wide enough. A dozen Bunnies were waiting just inside.

I *woof*ed and they scattered, zipping away to disappear into cracks and crevices in the stone wall. I stood guard as the guests went by, making their way to the stairs.

Calypso had recently made modifications to the minuscule machines with the intent of giving them more time between windings. These changes had resulted in what are referred to in certain circles as "unexpected consequences." I have observed three sorts of unexpected consequences at the Automated Inn.

The first is a delightful addition to the expected outcome. This is generally followed by the exclamation *"Eureka!"* and much rejoicing.

The second is a minor problem that manifests in addition to the solution the scientist was searching for. This is so common in the forward march of science that it elicits only a sigh.

The third is an outcome completely contrary to the inventor's intent. Such an outcome is frequently followed by the phrase "Flee for your life!"

The unexpected consequences of upgrading the Dust Bunnies were of the second sort. The Dust Bunnies did, indeed, need winding less often. But they now sang warlike operettas all night inside the walls, at frequencies far too high for human ears to hear, and they thumped and clanged. It may have sounded like plumbing problems, even to the other automatons, but dachshunds have excellent ears. The Dust Bunnies were up to something.

More troublesome still, they no longer waited for guests to remove their shoes or spectacles before they attempted to polish them. When President Roosevelt had come to the Inn to recruit the Kennewicketts as secret agents of the United States government, he had traveled disguised as a hobo. I shudder to think what the Bunnies might have done to the president's person if this adjustment had been made before his visit.

I had even caught three of them committing *intentional* acts of mischief. I referred to the troublesome trio as the Three Dustketeers, not only because of the cavalier hats with tiny brass feathers they had fashioned to match their tool belts, but for their too-frequent forays into derring-do. The term "derring-do" is used to describe actions that require a ridiculous amount of courage.

Dachshunds do *not* approve of derring-do, at least not when there is work to be done. Dust Bunnies, which are nothing but springs and cogs inside, should not be the least inclined to indulge in it.

If the three musketeers in Mr. Alexandre Dumas's books caused half as much trouble as this trying trio, I felt Cardinal Richelieu might be forgiven for trying to disband them. Only a fortnight before, I'd turned my

back for an instant and the Dustketeers had commandeered the coif of Contessa Maria Puzo.

A "contessa," as you no doubt know, is an Italian countess. The episode might have become an international incident had Calypso not styled a stunning new wig for the woman.

The tiny automatons seemed unusually docile today, not even peeking out until the last of the guests had followed Theoden and his great-grandmother down the hall. They emerged only as Wally unfastened my vest and hung it on its peg beside the door to the roof. (Calypso had forbidden flying inside the Inn the second time I became entangled in a chandelier.)

I looked back once to see the Three Dustketeers watching me as the others swarmed over my wings. They had apparently decided to polish, shine, and tighten screws between flights. As I hurried down the hall after Wally, I hoped it would keep them busy until after everyone had eaten.

You could be forgiven for mistaking Wally's room for a laboratory, or at the very least the machine shop of a mad scientist. It was full of gadgets, gears, and devices in various stages of construction or disrepair. Wally had his own area in his parents' lab, but it wasn't large enough to contain even half of the brilliant boy's contraptions.

Quite a lot of space was taken up at the moment by the newly oiled kite-folding machine. He had borrowed its construction concepts from Calypso's multihanded drafting mechanism. Wally's machine didn't draw—it folded, pleated, and tucked. It could pack the giant silk kite into an impossibly small package. It had to be monitored, however, because if it detected a single out-of-place wrinkle, it would start the whole process again. During the test phase of development, it had made Wally's bed sixteen times in a row.

I tugged Wally's tie from under a bag of explosive flash powder as he hung up his lab coat. The powder was used in the deployment device, and two of the steadiest hands of the folding machine measured a scant spoonful for each use.

"I feel it went exceptionally well, Noodles," he said as he put on the tie and twisted it into a four-in-hand knot. "Do you think they will purchase Theoden's photographs?"

I barked and wagged. How could anyone resist a picture of Wally Kennewickett?

"I hope so," Wally said. "We're planning on splitting the profits! I need funds for my research."

The boy genius hesitated before the designs he had drawn on the wall, took a piece of chalk from his pocket, and made a slight correction to a wing strut.

Wally could be absent-minded when he was inventing. He lost things. Like papers, and all sense of time and direction. But not even Wally could lose a wall. He chalked his best ideas there.

I whined, then tugged at his pants cuff before his mighty mind had time to fully engage in an act of invention. It was my duty to remind Wally of important things like brunch.

"You are right, Noodles," he said, putting the chalk back in his pocket. "We were to summon Mr. Tesla! But first, I must make a minor adjustment." He turned certain knobs on the folding machine, which would then adjust the angle of incidence on his kite's wings.

I gave his cuff one more tug, just to make sure he remained focused on brunch, then dashed ahead of him into the hall.

"Good morning, Walter!" the incredible inventor said when he answered the next door down. "Noodles!" He bowed. "Time to dine, I assume?"

Some might think it odd that Mr. Tesla would be shut in his room on such a busy day. The Kennewicketts understood that he required solitude. The Wizard of the West did not draw on walls—or anything else, for that matter. He formed *mental* images of his machines, testing every detail in his mind before he built them.

His devices always worked just as planned. Mr. Tesla felt that it saved time and money to invent in this way. *I* felt that such a feat was not possible for anyone but Mr. Tesla.

"Where has the morning gone?" he asked as we made our way down multiple flights of stairs. "I was just designing the last details of a certain device for your parents."

"Does it have to do with the tower, sir?" Wally asked.

Mr. Tesla smiled. "I'm afraid I can't discuss it without their permission! But — since we are alone — tell me more of this Iron Claw, Wally. You have described him as 'unnatural,' I believe?"

"Very unnatural,

sir," Wally said. During the Mesmers' recent attempted takeover of the Automated Inn, a fortuitous feather allergy had kept Wally from falling prey to the mesmerizing effect of Iron Claw's pinwheel eye.

The amazing boy had managed to produce anti-mesmerism goggles before Oliver, Calypso, and our fearless president returned to help him save the day. Calypso had later incorporated Wally's goggles into a popular line of hats.

"He spoke with a human voice," Wally went on. "My parents' theory is that this was a result of Madini's mind overpowering that of the bird."

"But that's not *your* theory?" Mr. Tesla queried.

"No, sir," Wally said slowly. "I believe the pigeon to have the more powerful mind."

I knew what courage it took for Wally to admit this. Kennewicketts tend to be exceedingly good or insanely evil. Mad Mars had been the insanely evil sort, and prone to peculiar theories. Wally's worst fear was turning into *that* kind of

Kennewickett. He'd never mentioned this fear to anyone, but he wrote about it in the journal he kept in his pocket.

The boy looked up earnestly at Mr. Tesla. "Do you think it is possible, sir?"

Mr. Tesla considered this for a moment. "Most certainly some planets are not inhabited, but others are, and among these there must exist life under all conditions and phases of development. Who is to say this Iron Claw is not a creature from some extraterrestrial coop?"

"Like the Martians in *The War of the Worlds*?" Wally cried.

I hoped that was not the case. Mr. H. G. Wells's book had been quite unsettling when we read it. I had hidden under the covers for weeks.

"Why not?" Mr. Tesla said. "I have always found pigeons to be friendly and kind, haven't you?"

"I couldn't say," Wally confessed. "I'm allergic, sir. They make me sneeze."

They were still discussing alien life when we

reached the dining hall, but with a nod from Mr. Tesla, they let the subject drop.

All thoughts of aliens fled my mind as we stepped through the door, and my knees went weak with anticipation.

Knives, the assistant cook, had prepared this feast, as Gizmo had been busy assisting Wally. As a result, there were a multitude of chopped, sliced, and diced dishes to choose from. Knives is quite proficient with the bladed attachments he uses in place of hands. There were tomato slices, boiled eggs cut like coins, thick slabs of bacon, and crisp julienned potatoes.

Talos, the footman, was circulating with platters of pastries Gizmo had baked before dawn; *dansk aebleskiver,* her famous Danish doughnuts; butterscotch sticky buns; popovers; scones; and pies.

Mrs. McDivit was sitting with her grandson, Mayor McDivit, and the members of the town council. I saw her slip a sticky bun into her purse.

"Hydrophoby bat!" she announced, pulling her skirts away as I hurried past.

Oliver, Calypso, Prissy, Theoden, and Mr. Jones were awaiting us at the Kennewicketts' table. After the ladies were seated, I took my place between Wally and his mother. Mealtime is my favorite time at the Inn. The food and company are always excellent.

I ignored the chip in my china plate—Suds, the dishwasher, apparently needed adjustment again—and focused my full attention on the pile of bacon at the center of the table.

"Where is Melvin?" Calypso asked, serving me two of the less significant bits of bacon and three slivers of egg. She had recently expressed concern about my girth.

"Girth" is the measurement around the middle of something. I didn't see how it could possibly be a problem when I felt so hollow inside.

"Freshening up," Prissy said. "He's refereed six games of lawn tennis already!"

As I took my first nibble, Melvin arrived, completely freshened and smelling slightly of Henkel's New Hair Pomade. I hated Henkel's. It numbed my nose.

"I have just come through the kitchen," Melvin announced, "where I found Knives serving brunch to a hobo!"

4

Wally looked up hopefully. I believe I have mentioned that President Roosevelt disguised himself as a hobo when he visited?

"Not *that* hobo." Melvin seemed unusually agitated. "An *actual* hobo."

"Whyever is he eating in the kitchen?" Wally's mother asked. "We have plenty of room at the table!"

Melvin glanced around, apparently concerned that the Kennewicketts had already invited the hobos who camped by the river to dine. Such persons were, in fact, scattered about the room. "We must stop feeding every indigent who stops by, Aunt Calypso!"

An "indigent" is a person too poor to provide

food or shelter for him- or herself. I am sure they are all too familiar with feeling hollow inside.

"Where would they eat, then?" Oliver asked. It was an excellent question. I believe I just mentioned the meaning of *indigent*?

"Explain to me, sir," Melvin said, ignoring his uncle's question and turning to Mr. Tesla, "the purpose of the expensive—er, I mean extensive tower you have attached to our roof?"

I slurped up a slice of egg. Something was clearly troubling Melvin. He kept glancing around the room in a most peculiar way. It was either a nervous fidget or a newly formed interest in his inheritance. His father, Wentworth Kennewickett, technically owned the Inn. Wentworth had left the building in his brother Oliver's care while he went about his travels. After Oliver married Calypso, they had transformed the frightening fortress into the Amazing Automated Inn. Melvin had never questioned its management or finances before.

Mr. Tesla exchanged a knowing look with the elder Kennewicketts.

"I have just finished the final component," he said, tapping his temple, "of the receivers."

"And it works?" Calypso queried. "You're certain?"

"Absolutely," the Wizard replied. "Would you pass the bacon?"

"What does it do?" Melvin asked more plainly.

"First things first." Oliver passed the platter past my nose. "I assume you have heard of the new phenomenon of wireless voice transmission, Melvin?"

Melvin nodded as Mr. Tesla helped himself to a magnificent mound of bacon.

"How the transmissions can be received even over the horizon from the sender has been a mystery. Calypso and I have been consulting with our colleagues Heaviside and Kennelly," continued Oliver, "who are about to publish a paper

proposing the existence of an electrically active layer in our upper atmosphere. They believe the transmissions hit this layer and bounce back to earth."

Mealtime at the Automated Inn is always educational. I helped myself to another bit of bacon.

"*We* refer to this electrically active area as 'the Heaviside layer,'" Calypso said, "which, I feel, is far more poetical than other names proposed."

Calypso believes that science and poetry have a great deal in common, such as beauty, structure, and identifiable patterns.

She nodded toward the Wizard of the West. "And this is where Nikola comes in."

"Thank you," Mr. Tesla said, accepting a delicious-looking buttery brown scone from Prissy. "My own unpublished experiments have proven not only that this 'Heaviside layer' exists, but that the earth beneath our feet functions as an enormous generator. My tower uses that generated energy to bounce a wave of a certain frequency off of the Heaviside layer."

"Whence," Calypso explained, "it can be picked up by the receiver Nikola has just conceived, and converted into electrical current."

I wagged. Scientists have long speculated that a mysterious medium called "aether" exists in the spaces between the solid matter in the universe. They believe aether to be capable of conveying and transforming energy.

"Such a receiver could be attached to any device that runs on electrical power!" Wally guessed. "Such as automatons!"

"Quite specifically automatons," Calypso said, setting her juice down. "They will be able to access the energy in the aether, and be free forever from their charging closets."

Jeeves went suddenly still as he considered the implications. Even the automatons, it appeared, had not guessed the secret of Mr. Tesla's tower.

Calypso clapped. "I do love surprises," she said.

She was just about to prove the point by putting one more slice of bacon on my plate when

Gizmo appeared. Her twitch was unfortunately in evidence as she rushed across the room.

"Gizmo?" Mr. Jones said, standing up. "Is all well?"

"M-m-madam," Gizmo began, "I—I—I . . ." She was shaking now, but she went on, "Waaaamuussnooootllll . . . k-k-k—"

The scent of overheating wiring was suddenly strong enough even for human noses to detect.

"Power down!" Calypso cried, dropping the bacon back onto the serving platter and rising from her seat. "Power down immediately, Gizmo! You are risking irreparable damage to your system!"

Mr. Jones was at Gizmo's side in one jump. The automaton's hand went to her head.

"No need, ma'am. It has ceased," she said, sounding slightly confused. "That has never happened before."

"I'll see you safely to the private parlor," Mr. Jones offered, taking Gizmo's arm. Jeeves took the other, and they led her away.

"I must excuse myself," Calypso said, setting her napkin down in order to go after them.

"Jones has it under control, my dear," Oliver replied. "I am certain he will see that Gizmo is safe. And," he added, looking pointedly around the room, "we risk introducing fear of mechanical malfunction in the guests if you rush away."

"Perhaps they *should* fear mechanical malfunction," Prissy pointed out. "Why can't we have a human butler like other people? Jeeves gives me the creeps!"

"If this were not an Automated Inn," her brother muttered, "would people be so eager to come here? I think not."

"Automatons are the Inn's most marvelous feature," Theoden agreed.

They made a good point. *I* felt the food was the true attraction—which was prepared by Gizmo and Knives. Calypso had completely forgotten the piece of bacon she had been about to give me. My nose inched toward a *dansk aebleskiver* on Wally's plate, but I recovered my self-control before it made contact. Dachshunds do not display bad manners, no matter the temptation!

"If Gizmo has suffered any harm, I will never forgive myself," Calypso said, sitting once more. "I knew her wiring needed updating even before we added to her responsibilities. I was waiting for Mr. Tesla's device to be complete. We must make certain modifications to the automatons if they are to draw electricity from the aether. I prefer to do it all at once."

"Speaking of your device, sir . . ." Melvin addressed Mr. Tesla. "Where will you install the meter?"

"There will be no meter," Mr. Tesla said simply. "The power will be free for anyone who can use it."

"Needless to say, not Edison, Westinghouse, or any of the other inventors working with current electrical models wishes such a device to exist," Oliver added with a touch too much enthusiasm. Oliver Kennewickett is fond of a fray.

"Great gobs!" Theoden exclaimed. "Imagine the impact on the war of the currents."

He was referring to the competition between Mr. Thomas Edison and Mr. George Westinghouse. Each had invested millions of dollars into the production of electrical power.

Edison had built the first electrical power-generation stations. They produced "direct current," which flowed through wires in one direction, much like water through a hose. Direct current could travel no more than a mile down a wire. Still, Edison had managed to light whole blocks of New York City with each generator.

But science could not, as the saying goes, stand still.

Westinghouse's newer generation stations produced "alternating current," which flowed first in one direction, and then in the other, almost faster than thought. Alternating current from a single generator could be carried hundreds of miles along power lines.

Wally was sure it would soon be used to light up even small towns such as Gasket Gully, reaching into each and every home. But it was more dangerous.

"It is true, I had not been able to find funding for this project," Mr. Tesla admitted. "Certain people would like to see it stopped."

"Aren't you afraid of filling the aether with electricity?" Theoden asked. "I can't get over what it did to that elephant!"

The war of the currents had grown very ugly

of late, very ugly indeed. In an attempt to discredit his competition, Edison had used Westinghouse's alternating current to electrocute an elephant.

"A despicable stunt intended to instill fear of Mr. Westinghouse's innovations," Calypso said scathingly.

Calypso believed that if great minds are not governed by great hearts, horrible things will happen.

"It was an act of showmanship," she went on, "and unworthy of a scientist!"

I had to agree. Elephants may not be as clever or as attractive as dachshunds, but no pachyderm should be made to pay the ultimate price simply so that Mr. Edison could make a profit.

"It isn't the electricity Mr. Tesla has to fear," Oliver added. "His device produces potential, not current. No. It's the investors who will try to stop him. Fortunes are at stake. Labs have been burned to the ground for less!"

"Then having it built puts the Inn at risk?" Prissy asked in alarm. "I feel our paterfamilias would not approve. In fact, I am certain of it!"

Prissy meant her own father, of course. A "paterfamilias" is a man who is the head of a family. Which would make Prissy's mother, Mame, the "materfamilias" of the Kennewickett clan.

"Wentworth would listen to logic," Oliver assured his nephew. "If electricity is free and freely available—"

"You could make millions selling electrical devices!" Theoden theorized. Melvin made a very strange sound.

"I was going to say 'humanity would benefit,'" Oliver replied, "but, yes, there will be profit to be made. Research must be funded, after all. Are you all right, Mel?"

"Yes, but there is something I must discuss with you," Melvin said, looking surreptitiously around the room again. "Immediately after brunch!"

At that moment, Talos appeared, carrying not pastries, but a letter on his silver tray.

5

Missive for you, ma'am," he said, bowing to Calypso.

"What is it, dear?" Oliver asked as she opened the envelope. "A request to present a scientific paper? An order for your amazing Mesmer-resistant bonnets?"

"No," Calypso said slowly. "An invitation from Contessa Maria Puzo to visit her in Peschiera, Italy! She does suggest I leave all Dust Bunnies behind, however."

Wally's fork wobbled. *"Arachne!"* he exclaimed.

"Gesundheit." Melvin glanced toward the window.

We all knew what he was looking for. Wally's

feather allergy had been advantageous in detecting pigeons in the past. Melvin was hoping his prize pigeons, the ones Madini had made off with, might still make their way home.

"Walter was not sneezing, Mel," Prissy said sadly. "He was referring to that eight-legged machine he has been ranting about."

"Monsieur Fevre's land yacht, *Arachne*," Wally agreed, producing his prized card so everyone could see. "The command deck is in her pseudo-cephalothorax—"

"Pseudo" means fake or false, and a "cephalothorax" is the portion of a spider to which the legs are attached. I had learned far too much about the architecture of arachnids recently.

"—And her abdomen houses a coal furnace that produces steam and rotates a turbine, which in turn produces the electricity that actually runs the yacht!"

"She'd need coal and water, then," Oliver observed. "Just like a steam locomotive."

"It does limit her," Wally admitted. "On land, the *Arachne* travels great distances only along railways, where coal and water are available at expected intervals."

The last article Wally had read to me had been particularly graphic in describing the shovel-tipped palpi the arachnid uses to scoop coal into her pseudo-mouth. "Palpi" is a word I would have been happy not to know. Palpi are the appendages beside the mouth of an arachnid. They use them to guide food into their gaping maw.

"She can travel by gas balloon as well," Wally enthused. "She emits it from her—"

"A fascinating process, Walter," Calypso said. "But perhaps not one to discuss at the table."

"Yes, Mother," Wally said.

Calypso is always considerate of tablemates' tastes.

"I have been reading about the *Arachne* myself," Oliver said. "Fevre's use of pressurized systems is fascinating. Her entire abdominal cavity is equipped with—"

"Must you mention her inner workings?" Prissy set down her spoon. "It's indelicate. Now I can't help but imagine the horrible thing crawling along the tracks. Stopping to feed on coal and suck a water tower dry. Then tipping her . . . her . . ."

"Abdomen," Wally offered. "Mother, the *Arachne* is in France, practically next door to Peschiera. We'd have to go right over her if we traveled by airship. I have been invited to tour her anytime!"

Prissy shuddered. "I have no desire to go back to Europe, if such creations crawl across the countryside! Though . . . we might arrange to meet with our parents, I suppose."

Melvin and Prissy are the products of prodigal parents.

A "prodigal" is someone who is wasteful, or spends extravagantly. Most of the money made by the Inn went to Melvin's paterfamilias.

Wentworth was heir to the Kennewickett fortune, after all. He had been traveling in Europe since before Oliver and Calypso were wed. I had never met the man.

"Can we go, Mother?" Wally asked.

"We could take the *Daedalus*," Oliver suggested. "After Nikola's project is completed, of course. I haven't seen Wentworth in ages. I'm sure he would appreciate the airship."

"A European tour does sound appealing," Calypso admitted. "I would like to show Wally a bit of the world. First things first, however. We have guests to attend to."

"Might I be excused, Mother?" Wally asked. "I must prepare for my next demonstration. Gizmo was going to fold the kite for me, but if she experienced a glitch—"

"Gizmo!" Calypso exclaimed. "I am sure Mr. Jones has the situation in hand, but really I have left her too long!"

"You wished to speak with me after the meal, Melvin?" Oliver said, standing up.

"I'm . . . I'm afraid I've forgotten what I was planning to say." Melvin blushed. "May I be excused?"

Regrettably, it was time to leave the table.

Theoden had to wait for Mrs. McDivit, but I followed Wally to his room, looking back only once at the food I was leaving behind. I did breathe deeply, but scent alone was not enough to sustain a dachshund until dinner. Still, I managed to keep pace with Wally as he raced up the stairs to his room.

I stopped just inside the door. Have you ever stepped into a room and been sure that someone had just left it? It was not just the disturbed dust motes spinning too quickly in the sunbeam. I tried to sort the scents, but the lingering smell of Henkel's New Hair Pomade still assaulted my nose. For a moment, though, I thought I could smell pigeon . . . and Madini.

I checked beneath the curtains for shoes, and under the bed for intruders. There were neither feathered fiends nor fiendish fakers to be found.

Perhaps my nose was merely confused by

the scent of hot wires. Gizmo's twitch must have gotten worse as she worked on the kite, leading to her odd behavior.

The device was perfectly packed and ready to go. Wally pulled on his lab coat and picked up the kite; then we hurried toward the belvedere.

The Dust Bunnies were nowhere in sight, but they *had* left my vest incredibly clean. The leather glistened and the brass shone bright. Wally set the kite down long enough to help me into it. I only hoped I had the strength to fly after such an insignificant brunch.

I was about to follow Wally onto the roof when I heard Theoden leading a new group of guests up the stairs below. As they climbed, he was offering to sell them photographic mementos of their day at the Inn. Mrs. McDivit was still with him. I could hear her shouting. I had just decided that I had best be in the air before she reached the roof when the Dust Bunnies began to sing.

I whirled to see one of the Dustketeers zip from behind a table leg—and then it was too late. The crowd was upon us. I stood politely aside, but the Dustketeer didn't. It leaped onto Mrs. McDivit's purse as she passed, and before I could bark a protest, it had disappeared inside. I could hardly pursue the pest into her purse, not when she already suspected me of having "hydrophoby"!

All I could do was watch and wait. Just before Mrs. McDivit stepped through the door, the Bunny reappeared and dropped a *dansk aebleskiver* to his waiting friends. The Dustketeers were plundering the pilfered pastries!

I was after them in a flash, but they managed to evade me by passing the pastry to other Dust Bunnies, as if we were engaged in a game of football along the length of the room. I skidded around a corner table and spotted the doughnut abandoned beneath a chair. Or so I thought.

I'd managed to wiggle my way to it when they swarmed over me. I found myself beset much as Gulliver in Mr. Swift's novel had been when he was set upon by Lilliputians.

I deliberately finished the *dansk aebleskiver*

before crawling from under the chair, then shook like a Labrador exiting the water. Dust Bunnies flew in all directions. *This* time they disappeared at my warning *woof*. I admit I was a bit more stern than usual.

I turned and raced out to the roof, feeling much less hollow inside. But I had no sooner launched myself skyward than I felt perhaps Calypso had a point. Surely one small scone could not weigh me down, but it was deucedly more difficult to fly.

I was past the parapet when I felt a tug on my left ear. I turned to see what it was and, naturally, my wings and wagger followed my nose. I flew in a complete circle before managing to straighten myself. Then, suddenly, my whiskers drooped and I was diving down the side of the Inn. My ears and whiskers had apparently developed a will of their own, twisting and turning me through the air!

And then the tugging and twisting stopped. I found myself hovering in front of a window— and discovered in my reflection the Three

Dustketeers perched upon my back. One was working my right ear, one my left, and the one in the center held reins attached to my whiskers. Those beastly Bunnies had not just been polishing my vest. They had been modifying it for their own amusement!

I was preparing myself for a spiral dive, determined to knock them from my back, when I realized we were outside Wally's room. And what I saw through the pane of glass turned my blood to ice.

A tall, thin, and menacingly mustachioed man was looking out at me. He had a pigeon perched upon his head. A pigeon with one dime-size eye patterned like a pinwheel.

The Mesmer Madini and Iron Claw were standing in Wally's room! Madini saw me and wiggled his fingers as if to say hello, then slid the window open just a hair.

"Now you will behold the vengeance of the Mesmers, disruptive dachshund," he said. "Your beloved Wally Kennewickett is doomed!"

Iron Claw spread his wings and laughed.

I saw a group of Dust Bunnies attack Madini's boots even as I smashed against the window in an attempt to get at the villains. But I only managed to knock myself half senseless and almost out of the air.

When I righted my tumble and rose again, the window was shut, and Wally's room was empty.

In a flash, I knew two things without a doubt:

The Dustketeers had shown me this on purpose.

And Gizmo's garbled words, "Waaaamuussnooootllll . . . k-k-k—" clearly meant, *"Walter must not launch his kite!"*

6

I wheeled, wagging frantically in an attempt to reach the roof before Wally pulled the lever that would send the kite aloft.

But I was too late.

The kite was racing skyward as my paws touched down next to him. I heard a harsh metallic clang, followed too quickly by a deafening explosion as the cable jerked to a halt. The shock wave knocked Wally from his feet and sent me tumbling to the base of Tesla's tower.

I landed on my back, all four paws in the air, and watched the remains of Wally's kite spreading above me like a firework gone wrong. I had failed him again. I tried to right myself, and realized why turtles have trouble turning over.

My wings were fixed in an open position,

preventing me from flipping to my feet. I wagged and wiggled wildly, but to no avail.

No one had noticed my arrival, and my presence was missed amid the chaos, but I did not whine. Dachshunds are known for their courage. Besides, I felt Wally's first thoughts should be for the safety of our guests. Fortunately, being farther from the blast, they had not been flung about. They were merely looking dazed and confused.

"Please exit the roof in an orderly manner," Wally instructed them as Jeeves helped him to his feet.

The phrase "in an orderly manner" means neatly and methodically. The good people of Gasket Gully apparently forgot its meaning the moment bits of watermelon began to rain down. They turned as one and rushed the door, not only holding it closed, but squishing old Mrs. McDivit against it.

"Jeeves, assist our guests!" Wally cried.

Jeeves achieved Walter's wish with astonishing

alacrity. The enormous automaton was through the crowd of guests in two jumps. He tucked Mrs. McDivit tenderly under one arm, and pulled the door from its hinges with the other.

"I told you he was going to blow something up," Mrs. McDivit announced as the concerned citizens rushed past her. "It's not over yet. *Mad Mars has returned! Flee for your lives!*"

Misinformation about Mad Mars aside, it was a very good plan, because the worst was still above us. The silk of the parachute had been blown into a billion flaming flakes that were settling more sedately than the watermelon rain.

Dachshunds do not like fire. I wagged wildly, but my wings would still not move and my legs could only wave in the air. I looked around for Wally, who had not missed me yet. He had leaped to help Theoden with his camera. They had just made it to the door when the fire began to fall.

I have mentioned courage; I am afraid mine fled me at that moment. I closed my eyes, willing myself not to whine or cry out. Because if I did, I was certain Walter Kennewickett would not hesitate to run into the falling flames to save me.

"Noodles?" Wally called. He had noticed I was missing! "Noodles!"

I opened my eyes to see the heroic boy racing across the roof toward me, his lab coat above his head. I had forgotten that Calypso uses only fireproof fabric in the lab coats she designs. Wally flung himself over me, pulling the marvelous coat around us both as flaming flakes settled from the sky.

We stayed in that position for a full minute before I sneezed. It wasn't flash powder, singed silk, or feathers that I smelled. It was burning hair. Wally lifted the corner of his coat and looked out.

"Great gobs!" he exclaimed. The fire was no longer falling, but Wally had not been the only one who had rushed to the rescue. Jeeves stood holding the bumbershoot over us. It had burnt to the metal ribs, and the brave butler's hair was ablaze.

It was at that exact moment that the guests lingering inside the belvedere started screaming.

"Great gobs!" Wally cried again, but even a boy genius can address only one disaster at a time.

He jumped to his feet and, using the wonderful coat once more, began to battle the flames on Jeeves's head just as Oliver and Calypso rushed through the now doorless portal onto the roof. Oliver instantly assessed the situation and leaped to Wally's aid. Between them, they managed to extinguish the butler.

"Walter! Are you injured?" Calypso queried over the cries from inside.

"No, Mother," Wally replied, brushing silk soot from his sleeve. "But our guests—!"

"Are being cleaned by Dust Bunnies," Oliver explained as Wally lifted me in his arms. "They may find it unsettling, but they will emerge unharmed."

Wally nodded.

"Noodles," the heroic boy whispered, "I almost forgot you. Are *you* all right?"

I licked his nose to assure him that I had emerged unscathed. It wasn't until Wally pulled off my broken vest that I realized that I, too, had forgotten someone.

The Three Dustketeers were no longer on my back! They must have been knocked loose by the force of the blast! I wriggled until Wally put me down; then I raced the length of the roof looking for the trio, dodging past Prissy, who had just arrived on the tumultuous scene. Mr. Tesla and Melvin were right behind her. All the other Dust Bunnies had gone downstairs with the screaming guests, and the Dustketeers were nowhere to be found. I returned to Wally's side.

The Wizard of the West had joined Oliver in examining the kitc reel, while Melvin and Prissy were surveying the damage from the blast. The entire roof was blackened, but so far as I could tell, there was not a single bit of Dust Bunny in sight.

"There was a wrench in the works!" Oliver announced as I peeked over the parapets, in case Iron Claw or Madini were clinging to the stone face. Nothing.

"I cannot believe you were so careless, Walter!" Prissy scolded. "Mr. Tesla's tower has been damaged!"

Oliver and Calypso exchanged a glance. They had clearly concluded that this was sabotage.

"We will pursue this in the private parlor, Priss," Calypso commanded, "after we've seen to our guests."

"Never mind my tower," Mr. Tesla said nobly. "I am just thankful that there were no casualties."

I fear he spoke too soon. As Calypso put her arm around Wally and turned him toward the doorway, I spied the missing Dustketeers at last.

The two who had tugged my ears were pulling their friend from the gutter into which they had tumbled. Both were battered and singed. The third, the one who had made reins of my whiskers, was hardly moving at all.

I approached the tiny automatons slowly, hoping they knew I wouldn't chase them. I need not have worried.

They laid their broken leader before me and chirped hopefully. I nudged him with my nose. I had no more than touched him when a spring sprang loose. I jumped back as it unwound, spinning the tiny automaton like a top.

And then the Dust Bunny lay very still. His unselfish act of derring-do had been his undoing. The other two zipped back and forth, squeaking in obvious alarm. I looked

around for help, but Calypso was leading Wally away.

I had never seen her so unsettled. Not only was Wally's hair standing up, but his lab coat was tattered, and Calypso didn't so much as mention it.

I snatched up the broken Bunny and dashed after them. Dachshunds do not leave the fallen behind, even if we are forced to carry them by the ear.

7

While dachshunds are the acknowledged kings of the canine form, there are disadvantages to our physiology.

"Physiology" is the way a living creature's body functions.

At the moment, I could think of only one disadvantage, and that was my inability to shout "Madini and Iron Claw were in Wally's room! The Mesmers have infiltrated the Inn! They are after Wally!"

However, I *was* able to sail down the stairs and career through the corridors, leaving the Dust Bunnies—save for the one I carried—with the Kennewicketts. I burst into Wally's room, but it was empty. When Wally defeated their last attempt at world dominion, Madini and Iron

Claw had disappeared amid a cloud of smoke, but there was no smoke here . . . just the scent I had detected before, and the unmistakable reek of pigeon. Since the miscreants had vanished, I raced back to Wally's side. At least I could watch over him.

We found ourselves in the private parlor much more quickly than I anticipated. The guests, apparently alarmed by Mrs. McDivit's claim of Mad Mars's return, had fled on foot down the harrowing road to the base of the mountain. Theoden had been dragged along against his will.

A certain member of the Kennewickett clan *paces* when perturbed. Oliver's traditional path across the parlor was north to south. Currently, Calypso was striding south to north, necessitating an occasional meeting in the middle.

Melvin and Prissy stood by the door, anxiously awaiting reports from Jeeves, Knives, and Talos, who had been sent in search of saboteurs.

Mr. Jones and Gizmo sat on the couch, while Mr. Tesla occupied a comfortable chair. Wally, slightly more kempt than he had been moments before, stood by his elbow. I was in Wally's arms, of course. In the rush to discover the evildoers, Wally alone had noticed the Dustketeer I carried. He was waiting for the opportunity to speak about it. Wally is very polite.

"Do we agree that my tower was the target?" Mr. Tesla asked quietly.

"Clearly a case of corporate sabotage!" declared Melvin.

No, no, no! The dastards were after Wally!

"We need facts," Oliver opined, as he almost collided with Calypso in the center of the room. "Do sit, dearest. We can't both pace. It is distracting!"

"I must do something to settle my mind," Calypso said. It was clear that she was very distraught. A curl had escaped from under her cap.

"Yes, but *I* pace," Oliver pointed out. "*You* tinker."

Wally cleared his throat, and everyone turned to us.

"If I may, Mother?" he began. "I believe Noodles has brought us a damaged Dust Bunny."

"That might fit the bill," Mr. Jones said, which meant it might be exactly what Calypso needed. I would have barked agreement if the undone Dustketeer had not been hanging from my mouth.

"Put it on the table, Noodles," Calypso commanded.

Wally set me down so that I could comply, and Calypso sank into a chair. I placed my front paws on the table and laid the Dust Bunny gently before her.

"His master spring has come unsprung," she said as I moved over a bit to let her work. "It's a very delicate device. I will need—" Oliver pulled a tiny toolkit from his hip pocket and set it beside her.

"And of course a magnifying glass," Calypso

went on. Oliver produced just such a glass from the inner pocket of his vest and handed it to Wally.

"He is also missing the cotter pins that held him together," Calypso observed.

Oliver made a performance of patting various pockets. I am a fan of pockets, especially those that hold cookies. I know where those pockets are usually located. But Oliver checked pockets in his pants, vest, and sleeves, then hidden pockets inside pockets, seeming to turn half his wardrobe inside out.

Watching the search seemed to settle everyone in the room. Finally, Oliver produced cotter pins—of the correct size—from the top of his boot.

"You're marvelous!" Calypso cried.

"Yes, dear," he said, and went back to his pacing.

Calypso bent over the tiny automaton. I noticed that the other Dust Bunnies had crept out to watch, sliding down the draperies and peeking from beneath furniture. The two remaining Dustketeers hopped up to the tabletop. I hadn't the heart to chase them away.

"Oh, look how cute they are!" Prissy cried.

"My Bunnies' behaviors are evolving in unexpected ways," Calypso admitted without looking up.

To "evolve" is to develop from something simple into something more complex. My feelings toward these particular Dust Bunnies had evolved a bit since I had realized that they were attempting to reveal the Mesmers' meddling to me.

Wally held the magnifying glass steady as his mother began the delicate operation. Calypso

was carefully untangling the steel spring when Jeeves, Knives, and Talos returned to report that no sign of the saboteur had been found.

"Probably slipped away with the guests," Mr. Tesla opined as Calypso rewound the wire onto a smooth wheel, which she handed to Gizmo.

Then, moving more speedily, she lifted the Dust Bunny's breastplate and set about adjusting tiny levers, flywheels, cogs, and gears.

Finally, she took the master spring back from Gizmo, tucked it inside the Dust Bunny, and clipped him together with the cotter pins.

The room erupted in Dust Bunny cheers as he teetered upright, though the Kennewicketts couldn't hear them. The Dust Bunny wobbled once, hopped around the table, and stopped in front of my nose. I hoped he was not going to be too sentimental. Dachshunds are very humble. We do not expect thanks for our good deeds.

He tottered, then reached up slowly—and grabbed my sore whiskers. He gave them a terrific yank, then zipped away. I was after the rascal in a flash, but the Bunnies disappeared, as was their wont, before I could catch a single one.

"As was their wont" means "as they usually do."

"Now," Oliver said when they were gone, "shall we consider the conundrum with refreshed minds?"

"First things first," Calypso said, brushing away her curl. "Hair, Walter! And attend your shirttail."

I watched with relief as Wally combed his hair and tucked in his shirt. Calypso was quite herself again.

"Now," she said when he was done, "what do you remember?"

Wally frowned. "I had adjusted the angle of incidence three degrees in an attempt to accommodate the high winds."

"It was an exceptional launch," Gizmo agreed. "Though old Mrs. McDivit was causing a commotion."

"You don't suppose she had anything to do with it?" Prissy asked.

"No," Wally said. "She was at brunch until just before the launch."

That was true. She had been filling her purse with pastries!

"Perhaps we should focus on the kite and the cannon, Walter," Oliver suggested.

"Yes, Father," Wally said. "Prissy summoned us to brunch, and I asked Gizmo to refold the kite for me. I recalibrated the folder when I stopped in my room."

Gizmo suddenly stood up. "I have no record of any events in Wally's room," she said. *"I don't remember folding the kite."*

"Then the place to begin our investigation," Calypso concluded, "is Walter's room."

I rushed ahead, hoping that Madini had left a trace I had not yet discovered, or that Iron Claw had shed a feather. The Kennewicketts had to know the full extent of this disaster as soon as possible.

Wally opened the door carefully and looked both ways before he stepped inside.

Calypso examined the kite-folding contraption while Oliver ignited a pinch of the flash powder to make sure it had not been replaced with something more potent.

Melvin and Prissy checked in the closet and under the bed.

Gizmo stood beside Wally in the center of the room.

"Do you remember anything?" Wally asked.

"No," Gizmo said.

Wally turned around once . . . twice . . .

"What is he doing?" Melvin asked.

"Observing," Mr. Tesla explained. "A scientist must be as meticulous as any detective in his observations!"

Wally's head tipped as he considered his calculations on the wall. He strode to them, and I immediately realized what had attracted his attention. The chalk of his most recent diagram was smudged. Above the smudge were five blots, as if the fingers and palm of a large hand had pressed against the stone. Wally matched his hand to the print, and shoved.

The wall swung open.

8

My hackles rose. Wally had discovered the mechanism by which the Mesmers had managed to disappear! I was certain of it. The passage smelled of pigeon.

Mr. Tesla studied the dark doorway, rubbing his chin.

"Oliver," Calypso began, sounding slightly chagrined, "were you aware we had secret passages within our walls?"

"I was not," Oliver admitted. "Gizmo? Where does this lead?"

Gizmo blinked, whirring softly as she checked the plans stored in her mechanical mind. "This passage is not on the official floor plan. Or . . . if it was, it has disappeared from my data. Perhaps I should resign as security chief, sir!"

"Let's not be hasty." Mr. Jones stepped closer to the automaton. "We'll sort this out."

"I—*ah-ah-ah-choo-choo-choo!*" Wally was seized by a series of sneezes. "I meant 'I agree,' of course," he said when he recovered. "I'm sure you shouldn't resign, Gizmo. *Ah-choo!*"

I leaped into the darkness, eager to sniff out the cause of Wally's distress. With any luck, I wouldn't need words to inform the Kennewicketts of Iron Claw's presence. Wally's allergies would do it for me.

I hadn't gone far before I picked up the fowl scent and followed it to its source. The Dust Bunnies had managed to pluck plumage from Iron Claw even as he made good his escape.

It hadn't been pretend battles I'd heard raging behind Wally's wall. They had been real, and probably terrible. The Dustketeers had detected the Mesmers' presence and established a resistance force. The minuscule machines had been guarding Walter Kennewickett while everyone slept! An unexpected emotion swelled my heart. I was not alone in the knowledge that Iron Claw had infiltrated the Inn. I had minions, and they were on the job!

I snatched up the feathers and bounded back to Wally's side.

"Wha-*ah-ah-choo!*" the boy genius said. "I meant 'What have you got'—*ah-choo!*—I meant 'there,' of course!"

Calypso collected the offending feathers and flung them out the window.

"Those were Columbidae rectrices!" Prissy cried.

"And 'rectrices' would be?" Wally asked. I was glad he made the inquiry. I had never encountered the term before.

"Tail feathers," Mr. Tesla said grimly. "Most birds have twelve. They enable the bird to brake in midair or control the direction of flight."

Wally reached for his pocket journal. The importance of tails seemed to be a recurring theme in the perpetual puzzle of flight, which he hoped to solve.

Wally had designed my winged vest

after reading an article about Percy Pilcher's man-size glider the *Hawk*. Pilcher had plunged to his death when the *Hawk*'s tail failed. Tail failure seemed to be a common element in many aerial disasters. I had suffered one myself during my first flight, but my wagger had been performing magnificently since then. I hoped Wally was contemplating changes to his man-lifting kite and not to my flying device. Dachshunds are proud of their tails; I did not want mine festooned with feathers!

"Iron Claw's, I expect," Mr. Jones intoned as Wally made his note. "If the mesmerizing bird has been here, can Madini have been far behind?"

Melvin shoved his hands into his pockets. I knew he still had nightmares about the Mesmers' last visit. I had heard him cry out in the night.

"Something caught Iron Claw by the tail," Prissy said, not noticing her brother's pallor.

"He might have dropped one feather naturally, but not three!"

"Something plucked his plumage?" Oliver asked.

Something indeed. I looked around the room. There were no Dust Bunnies in sight. I hoped they were hounding the dastards through the secret passages even as Oliver spoke.

"Columbidae are the only birds that can release their whole array of tail feathers if caught," Prissy explained. "They eventually grow back."

"Riddles wrapped in mysteries, tucked into conundrums," Oliver said.

"But why should the Mesmers care about Mr. Tesla's tower?" Prissy asked.

"Because," Calypso conjectured, "our automatons are immune to their interference. Providing Gizmo and the others with an uninterruptible power supply is key to the task presented to us by the president."

"We did agree to save the world," observed Oliver. "And our president is depending on us."

"We will save the world by doing what we do

84

best," Wally guessed. "Creating and employing technology."

"Technology" is the science of mechanical and industrial arts.

"It has been Oliver and Calypso's plan all along," Mr. Tesla explained, "to free the automatons from their charging stations so that they could assist in confronting the Mesmers anywhere in the world. Your parents invited me to stay at the Inn as a safe place to develop my invention."

"Safe from the Mesmers?" Prissy inquired.

"And from industrial sabotage and spies," Tesla admitted. "I have received threats before. My invention would unsettle the world. Powerful people would lose large amounts of money if electricity were free."

"It's a pity these passages are not supplied with electricity," Oliver said.

"I have candles, Father." Wally whirled toward his desk. "The miscreants may be making their way through these tunnels still!"

He provided a candle for each member of

the party. Oliver produced a box of Delightful, Dependable, and Safe Matches, his own invention. Calypso would not allow the use of the white phosphorus matches that anyone could buy at the five-and-dime. White phosphorus is poisonous.

Oliver's matches were not poisonous. But they were not necessarily safe, despite their name. Their spark and smoke usually announced that something exciting was imminent—such as a skyrocket gone sideways or a minor explosion. I didn't desert my post by Wally's side, but I did cover my nose with both paws as the first match was lit.

I worried for naught. Nothing but candle-wicks were set aflame, and in two shakes of my tail, we were ready to explore.

I kept a close eye on Wally as we stepped through the door. In the light of the candles, I could see that the passage was dust-free and extremely tidy.

That would be the work of the Bunnies.

We turned right, and walked past peepholes

that peered out of portraits into bedrooms and halls, and then followed our noses down multiple stairs until a final door opened and we were standing in the dungeon lab. To my disappointment, the Dustketeers joined us there.

Their presence could only mean that the Mesmers had made good on their escape.

"This explains my missing papers," Oliver said, swinging the secret door open again, "but not where the Mesmers have gone."

We climbed the stairs once more and, when we reached Wally's room, we turned left. The passage wound through the walls until it ended at last in a secret library. The room's ominous air was heightened by a mummified rat, which hung from the chandelier.

Shivers slithered down my spine. Dachshunds are known for their dauntless spirit. But it is exceedingly unsettling to find such things inside the walls you have always thought kept you safe. I feared that there were still darker secrets to be discovered.

Calypso requested that the rat remains be

removed before we explored the room. Wally borrowed Melvin's kerchief and, after stacking several books on the large library desk, was able to reach the wretched rodent. The rat, wrapped in a monogrammed shroud and smelling of Henkel's New Hair Pomade, was whisked away by the doughty Dustketeers.

"Doughty" means brave and persistent. The more I observed my minuscule minions, the more I realized that bravery and persistence had somehow worked their way into their gears. This wasn't surprising. No one could spend time with the Kennewicketts—Oliver, Calypso, and Wally, that is—without some of their amazing qualities rubbing off.

After the Dustketeers had gone, I assisted Calypso in searching the corners and crevices for any sign of more rats, dead or alive.

Oliver picked up a peculiar marble from a pedestal atop the ancient desk.

Gizmo, Mr. Jones, and Mr. Tesla opened a cupboard and uncovered designs of Mad Mars's

Folly, as the building was called before it became the Automated Inn.

"These are more complete than the copies currently contained in my cranium," Gizmo concluded after studying them for a moment. "The Inn is a warren of secret ways!"

A "warren" refers to the underground home of rabbits, with burrows running in all directions. I checked under a chair for more rats.

"Walter," Prissy began, peeking behind a scarlet drapery, "when did you pose for a portrait?"

She pulled a cord, and the drapery swung aside. I found myself gazing up at a magnificent image offset by gleaming gold molding.

My first thought was: *Wally has been framed.* My second was: *Why is he petting that very large bat?*

"It's my grandfather," Oliver marveled, holding his candle high. "Mad Mars himself, as a boy. This must have been his private study!"

"So he really did keep bats," Prissy whispered. "Just like Mrs. McDivit always says."

"Grandfather was allergic to feathers," Oliver explained. "But he loved anything with wings."

Wally's hand went to the pocket over his heart, the one in which he kept his journal. I licked the fingers of his other hand, but he didn't seem to notice. He stood frozen before the portrait. Discovering such a remarkable resemblance to his evil ancestor must have been worse than finding dead rats in the walls. Much worse.

"Bats were the obvious choice for pets," continued Oliver.

Calypso cleared her throat, and Oliver glanced at her.

She nodded toward Wally.

"He wasn't always *Mad* Mars, you know," Oliver said quickly. "He was a very decent sort once. Fond of furry creatures."

"Even after he went mad," Mr. Jones agreed. "It took a great deal of effort to become feared by friend and foe alike. And a great deal of study, apparently." He began pulling books from the shelf. "*Growing Your Fortune Through*

Skullduggery, How To Use Friends and Manipulate People, and *Dubois's Guide to Dungeon Design."*

"There are Kennewicketts, and then there are Kennewicketts!" Prissy folded her arms.

"What do you mean?" Gizmo asked.

"I believe a Kennewickett ordered you to alter the kite," Prissy pronounced. "The evidence is clear: Madini has meddled with Wally's mind. After the first launch, Wally returned to his room. I believe Gizmo discovered him there rigging the blast to destroy the tower. He ordered her not to tell. We all know what happens if an automaton attempts to disobey a direct order from a Kennewickett."

Its wiring would melt!

Gizmo gasped, and her hand lifted to her head again.

"Not possible," Mr. Jones said flatly.

"It really isn't, dear," Calypso concurred. "Wally's allergic to Iron Claw. It is a quirk that saved him from Madini in the past."

Calypso was correct, of course. But Prissy *was* onto something. The hot metal scent in

Wally's room *could* have been Gizmo's wiring shorting out. However, Prissy couldn't have known that my keen dachshund nose had picked up another scent there as well. *Henkel's New Hair Pomade.*

Melvin Kennewickett was the mole!

I bared my fangs, preparing to bite.

"Walter didn't do it, Priss," Melvin said before I could lunge. "I did."

Melvin wobbled from the weight of his confession. He looked so pale I feared he would collapse.

"My brother Wentworth has been mesmerized, hasn't he?" Oliver exclaimed as he took Melvin's arm and led him to a chair. "And the Mesmers are holding him captive." Prissy gasped, while Mr. Tesla and Calypso exchanged puzzled looks.

"How did you know, sir?" Melvin asked as he collapsed onto the cushions. "How could you possibly know?"

Oliver nodded in Prissy's direction, "I suspected Gizmo had encountered an errant

Kennewickett as well. Excellent detective work, Priss!"

"All except the part about Walter," Mr. Jones pointed out. "But out with it, Oliver! How *could* you know your brother had been mesmerized?"

"To start with, my nephew, Melvin, has a very expressive face," Oliver said, turning to the young man. "When we entered Wally's room, you looked as if you were in a state of shock. I couldn't conceive of what had caused it until I found this!"

He held up the marble he had taken from the desk. "Wentworth's prize shooter. My brother must have found his way here when he was a boy. He was impossible to find when we played hide-and-seek. Wentworth has always been good at games and incomparable at keeping secrets. The only way Madini and his feathered friend could have found their way into these secret passages is if my brother had been mesmerized and given them the information!"

"But how did you become involved, Melvin?" Calypso asked.

Melvin swallowed and squared his shoulders. "I stumbled across Madini and Iron Claw when I went to investigate mysterious noises emanating from Wally's room," Melvin admitted. "I covered my eyes to avoid being mesmerized, and attempted to call for help." His voice was shaking. "Madini put his hand over my mouth. And then he told me exactly what he intended to do: The explosive device was not aimed at the tower. It was meant to destroy Walter. The Mesmers have vowed to take vengeance on him."

"But surely you could have warned Walter somehow!" Calypso cried. "You could have told Oliver or myself!"

I realized the rumble I heard was coming from my own throat.

"I . . . I tried," Melvin said, growing paler still. "I did, Aunt Calypso. But the evil magician made it clear that my parents would pay the ultimate price if I dared to meddle in Mesmer affairs. Still, I snuck back into Walter's room and removed as much explosive powder as I dared. Then I hurried to brunch, determined to find some way to alert you—oh, why should anyone believe me now?" Melvin's head sank in despair.

"I believe you," Mr. Jones announced. "If I am not mistaken, Melvin, you had gathered your courage and started to speak when Talos arrived with the contessa's invitation."

"Yes!" Melvin's head lifted.

"And when Walter said *Arachne*," Calypso guessed, "you thought he sneezed. Which would have meant Iron Claw was near. Perhaps outside the window . . . or listening from within the walls!"

"Yes." Melvin looked miserable. "That's when I lost my courage. Gizmo saw me in Wally's room removing the flash powder, and I . . . I commanded her not to tell. I didn't fully realize the harm it would do to her mind."

"Surely the Mesmers will have figured out that you meddled, Mel!" Prissy burst into tears. "Our parents are doomed!"

"Now, dear, we mustn't assume the worst," Calypso said, offering a lace handkerchief to her sobbing niece before she turned to Oliver. "We must organize a rescuc immediately!"

"Agreed." Oliver had begun to pace again, his marvelous mind already at work.

"You saved my life by removing the explosives, Mel," Wally said firmly. "We will save your parents!"

I jumped out of the way as Oliver rcversed direction.

"We need more information," he said. "Where are Wentworth and Mamc being held? If the automatons have managed to capture Madini—"

Just then, two Dust Bunnies led Talos and Jeeves into the library. It was quickly becoming impossible to stay out of the way of every foot in the room. Wally scooped me up, and I licked his ear. It is good to have friends in high places.

"The miscreants have eluded us once more, sir," Talos announced.

"They are gone, sir," Jeeves agreed.

Prissy sank to the floor. "How can we save

97

Mother and Father? Not even Mr. Jones has been able to discover the Mesmers' hideout. And they've disappeared again, leaving no clues behind!"

"They've left one," Wally said.

Everyone turned to stare at the astute boy.

"Signore Giuseppe," he said simply. "In Italy."

q

o you mean that our parents could be cooped up in Italy?" Melvin cried.

"It is possible." Oliver paused to consider. "The research papers Signore Giuseppe published were whisked away through these passages."

"And my investigations have confirmed that this Giuseppe is famous for his pet pigeons," Mr. Jones added.

"The pigeons of Italy are wonderful birds," Mr. Tesla mused. "I can't believe this monster is roosting among them!"

"You must admit there is strong circumstantial evidence, Nikola," Calypso said.

"Circumstantial evidence" is a fact or facts that allow you to draw a logical conclusion long before you have hard evidence. The brilliant deductions made by Sherlock Holmes are based on his excellent grasp of circumstantial evidence.

"They must be saved!" Mr. Tesla declared.

"Our parents?" Melvin asked.

"Them too!" Mr. Tesla turned toward the door. "I must go to Italy at once!"

I believe I have mentioned Mr. Tesla's fondness for pigeons? Even the greatest of men have their occasional eccentricity.

An "eccentricity" is a strange or unusual behavior. Dachshunds are *never* eccentric.

Oliver had stopped pacing. "If you plan on saving the pigeons, Nikola, you will need our help. And we will need your help to save my brother as well."

"Forgive me," said the Wizard of the West. "I am at your service, Kennewicketts. The thought of birds being abused had driven me momentarily mad. What is the plan?"

"We *all* go to Italy," Calypso said. "As Walter cleverly concluded, it is our only clue. But we must prepare first."

"Ahem." Mr. Jones cleared his throat. "I'm sure it has occurred to everyone that Wally is in great danger if he accompanies you?"

Mr. Jones was right. Wally *had* been the target of the Mesmers' attack.

"You will be traveling into the Mesmers' lair, as it were," Mr. Jones went on. "Walter might be safer with me, masquerading as my nephew. What do you say, Wally? Do you want to learn to drive a train?"

Wally's arms tightened around me. I knew it wasn't fear that drained the color from the brave boy's face. It was the possibility of being left behind while the rest of the Kennewicketts rushed to the rescue.

"Thank you, sir," Wally said politely. "But I would prefer to pursue the villains to their lair!"

"Quite right," Calypso approved. "The whole world is in danger until we have dealt with the evildoers."

"It might be obvious that you are onto them if you all travel to Italy," added Mr. Jones.

"Not if we appear to be responding to the

contessa's kind invitation,"—Calypso straightened Oliver's collar and brushed a cobweb from his hair—"which I coincidentally received at brunch!"

Oliver turned to Mr. Tesla. "How quickly can you repair your tower?"

"I will need three weeks at least," the Wizard said. "And if I spend my time on the tower, I will not be able to finish the receivers with which to modify the automatons."

Gizmo and Talos exchanged a glance, and Jeeves's grimace grew even grimmer.

"The automatons are essential to our success," Calypso said. "They must be freed from the need to recharge nightly. We can work on the receivers and install them on the way."

"But madam," Gizmo began, "if we all go, we will leave the Inn unattended!"

"*Tsk*," Mr. Jones said. "If I can't look after Walter, at least let me take care of the Inn!"

I wagged. Not only was Mr. Jones one of the rare humans immune to Iron Claw's mesmerizing eye, he was sure to leave the Inn smelling of snickerdoodles!

"Can you manage alone, sir?" Wally queried.

"Oh, I won't be alone," Mr. Jones assured him.

"You mean your alleged Irregulars?" Melvin queried. "But we have never seen them, sir!"

People perpetually doubt Mr. Jones. I believe it is a result of his relentless pursuit of conspiracy theories.

"Pardon me," Gizmo said, coming to stand next to the engineer, "but I believe you met Billy in the kitchen. He is a top-notch Iron Road Irregular."

"The *hobo?*" Melvin asked.

"Excellent disguise, isn't it?" Mr. Jones patted his portly sides.

"Most people go out of their way to ignore hobos," Oliver said thoughtfully.

It was true. Even President Roosevelt, with one of the most famous faces in the world, had traveled undiscovered while dressed as a hobo.

"But not you." Mr. Jones beamed. "You are by no means without friends, Kennewicketts, though many of your friends appear to be without means."

"Are you implying that you would invite hobos into the Inn?" Prissy gasped.

"Priss," Melvin said, "it might help save our parents."

"We'll invite only those of excellent character," Mr. Jones assured her.

Oliver nodded. "Indigence is not always an indication of ill breeding," he said. "It can be the mark of misfortune, or simply a call to adventure. I don't suppose *we* could travel as hobos—"

"Oliver," Calypso said before he could finish the thought, "we must take the *Daedalus*. Time is of the essence"

"Speaking of time . . ." Mr. Jones consulted his pocket chronometer. "I've got a train to catch and people to contact!" He took Gizmo's small hands in his own work-worn mitts. "Chin up, Gizzy! We'll sort this out soon enough; you'll see. We'll be making pfeffernüsse by Christmas!"

"Your recipe or mine?" Gizmo inquired with a curious catch in her voice.

I'm sure I was not the only one who noticed that the automaton's hands lingered in those of the engineer.

"Ahem," Oliver said. "I believe we should apprise the president of the attack, as well as our travel plans, as soon as possible."

To "apprise" means to tell someone about something. I started toward the door. Oliver was right. Theodore Roosevelt would be pleased to know his secret agents were on the move!

"I should send word to my family in Serbia," Mr. Tesla said, "and tell them I am coming for a visit. That will be good cover as well."

"I'll send the telegrams at my next stop," Mr. Jones offered, releasing Gizmo's hands at last.

With a plan in place, we exited the hidden

library and hurried through the secret passageways. Wally set me down, but I stayed close by his side, Mr. Jones's words echoing in my ears: *Wally is in great danger* . . .

I saw him glance worriedly at the portrait of Mad Mars as we left the room.

I did not let my best friend out of my sight for the next three weeks. I dogged his every step as he made sure the six fashionable hats with anti-Mesmer goggles—one for each Kennewickett and one for Mr. Tesla—were ready for the final confrontation. I followed along while he helped Jeeves replace the belvedere door that had been torn from its hinges, assisted Mr. Tesla with the work on his tower, helped Oliver with the filling of special Voltage Vats that would power the *Daedalus* if the wind failed us, and ran errands for Calypso and Gizmo as they saw to the provisioning of the aerostat.

Dachshunds are blessed with short legs. I now believe that this is to encourage us in the pursuit of flight. But since Calypso would not allow the wearing of wings inside the Inn, my legs had to carry me up and down halls and stairs in pursuit of Wally.

Fortunately, the frequent errands forced us to stop by the kitchen often. I could never have made it through a day without snacks.

I was enjoying a lovely lamb chop there as Wally discussed the fine points of our preparations with Gizmo when the first of the Iron Road Irregulars arrived.

The dusty hobo walked right in the back door, his hat in his hands.

"Jones said you might have a spare pfeffernüsse or two," the tattered man said.

"Walter," Gizmo said, "may I present Billy? Billy, this is Walter Kennewickett."

"Pleased to meet you, sir," Wally said. "Won't you come in? I'm sure we can find you a cookie."

"Billy's request for a pastry is a code arranged by Mr. Jones," Gizmo explained. I had never seen an automaton blush before. She turned to Billy. "This may be uncomfortable, sir, but it is necessary." She clapped twice.

Dust Bunnies I had not even suspected were lurking zipped out of secret hiding places, clambered up his legs, and even dropped to his head from the chandelier.

"Would you mind showing our guest to his room, Walter?" Gizmo asked. "The Bunnies will take care of everything."

"Follow me, sir," Wally said as the Dust Bunnies went to work. By the time we reached our new guest's room, the gentleman who followed Wally could hardly be recognized. Not only had his hair been trimmed, his boots cobbled, and his coat mended, but there was an enormous smile on his face.

"William Williams," he said with a bow, "at your service! What do you think, old boy?"

"Perhaps the posy . . . ?" Wally ventured.

"A bit much?" William plucked out the daisy the Bunnies had tucked like a boutonniere into his neatly stitched buttonhole. "Agreed. When do we eat?"

"Dinner is served at seven, sir."

"Excellent!" the dapper dandy said with a flip of his now fastidious hat. "I can hardly wait!"

More Irregulars arrived on every train, and the Dust Bunnies kept transforming them, until the Inn was almost full. All of Mr. Jones's Irregulars appeared to be of the "seeking adventure" sort. Upon tidying them up, the Dust Bunnies had unearthed an errant heir, a pie maker, six musicians, one accountant, and even a professor or two.

I pondered that point while Wally repaired my wings.

Were only Mr. Jones's hobos the seeking adventure

types? Or were *all* hobos someone special in disguise? I suspected that the Kennewicketts adhered to the "someone special" theory.

To "adhere" means to stick fast to something. The Kennewicketts stuck fast to their constant kindness to hobos.

Just days before our departure, Wally pleaded with Calypso to allow him to bring his kite and rail cannon along so that he could continue his experiments. She agreed, but not before checking his bolt system to make sure the heavy cannon would remain secured to the ship even in the wildest storm.

At last, the day came when occupants of the Inn gathered on the roof where the *Daedalus* was docked. It was time to say goodbye. Mr. Jones arrived just before departure, bringing a message from Theodore Roosevelt.

Bully! the president wrote. *Godspeed, Kennewicketts. Edith and I have many friends in Europe. Expect they'll want to help along the way. —TR.*

"I hope he does not mean Monsieur Fevre,"

Prissy said as Mr. Tesla followed her aboard. "I do not want help from a spider!"

Mr. Jones turned to Gizmo. "We'll keep things running, Gizzy," he assured her. "I know you need that tower."

"Depend on us, Kennewicketts!" the Irregulars called. "Don't worry about a thing. Just save the world!"

"And the pigeons," Mr. Tesla added.

The Dust Bunnies lined the parapet to wave goodbye as the *Daedalus* slipped into the sky.

10

The land below us was a gorgeous green counterpane stitched together by road and rail. If the winds were favorable, Oliver planned to maintain an altitude of fifteen hundred feet all the way from Gasket Gully to New York City, where we were to turn east over the Atlantic Ocean.

There, the winds at higher altitudes over the water would move us along more quickly. The Voltage Vats would power the propellers when the winds were not favorable. Mr. Tesla planned to build a receiver to replace the vats as a power source just as soon as all of the automatons had been updated.

Traveling aboard the aerostat always made Wally even more keen to conquer heavier-than-air powered controlled flight. I stayed close by his side. I wasn't only wary of evil pigeons. Wally had been known to walk into windows or step into space when caught up in a conundrum. This tendency was extremely dangerous on an airship. The deck of the *Daedalus* had railings all around, but I knew Calypso was counting on me to watch over her son.

After we left Gasket Gully, Wally managed to launch his man-lifting kite only twice. The weather was unusually mild, with barely enough wind in the lowlands to keep it aloft. Once we reached the ocean, the aerostat would rise to five thousand feet, and the kite would not be able to fly at all. The winds above us would be so strong, they would rip out the bolts that fastened the steel reel to the deck.

I could tell that this was a disappointment to the boy scientist. He had hoped to complete several experiments before we left land. Calypso assured him, however, that the winds above Spain, which we would have to pass over on the way to Italy, should be wonderful at this time of year.

In the meantime, Wally assisted Oliver in taking atmospheric readings of all sorts.

Every mealtime was spent discussing plans and tactics that might be of use against Madini, but Wally was strangely quiet. He hadn't mentioned his theory about Iron Claw since Prissy had unveiled the portrait of Mad Mars. In fact, he hadn't said much about Mesmers at all.

Twice a day, I made my rounds. Patrolling the aerostat did not take as long as patrolling the entire Automated Inn, which left me lots of time to worry. Even if I no longer had a mole to discover, the Mesmers were proving more devious than even I had imagined. How does a single dachshund defend his best friend against an evil organization with masterminds, mesmerizing powers, and minions galore? One night, I was watching over Wally as he slept and considering my conundrum when I heard a tiny, tinny tune.

Stowaways!

I followed the sound and discovered the Dustketeers on deck, crooning to the silvery moon. I sat down to watch as it rose over the horizon. There were no guests for them to annoy and no coifs to commandeer, after all. And I felt much less alone with them beside me.

Suddenly, their night song stirred my soul, waking the blood of ancient ancestral wolves that still runs thick in dachshund veins.

I tipped my muzzle to the sky and had a good howl before heading back to my warm bed. I felt much better as I burrowed under the blankets beside Wally.

On the third day, we passed above New York City and headed out over the ocean, rising to a higher altitude and, to Melvin and Prissy's relief, gaining speed.

Calypso and Mr. Tesla set about assembling the small devices that would allow the automatons to access electricity from the aether. One by one, the mechanical men and women were invited into the lab and stepped out freed from the need to draw power from the Voltage Vats each night. I believe I have described "unintended consequences"? I should have known that something as marvelous as being freed from wires and batteries was certain to come with a few.

Gizmo could not stop smiling, and she skipped about the ship. Jeeves was as grim and efficient as ever, but there was an unsettling sparkle in his eye. Knives, freed from the necessity of spending hours each night charging, took up whittling during his free time. The Dustketeers delighted in cleaning up the curlicues of wood, catching them as they fell. Talos was everywhere, learning acrobatic tricks from Prissy, judo from Wally, and lawn tennis swings from Melvin. Suds developed a taste for watching clouds and daydreaming. She had to be constantly reminded to do the dishes.

We had crossed most of the mighty Atlantic,

and Mr. Tesla was working on the last receiver—the one for the *Daedalus* herself—when the weather turned against us and the winds died. For the first day of the calm, the *Daedalus* sailed on, propellers powered by the reserve in the Voltage Vats. But when the vats were empty at last, we hung motionless above the waves. Puffy cumulus clouds huddled like lazy sheep all around us.

"If I didn't know better," Calypso commented on the third day, "I would think we were in the doldrums!"

The "doldrums" are an area of ocean near the equator where the wind is sometimes so still it traps sail-powered ships for days or even weeks.

Oliver checked his instruments and looked longingly at the altostratus clouds two thousand feet above us. They were scudding merrily across the sky, practically scampering along on the strong upper wind. But the *Daedalus* could not rise above five thousand feet. The air was thinner at higher altitudes, and would cause the helium gas to expand and leak from her hull.

Wally whiled away the hours by testing variations on Oliver's explosive powders, sending up small clouds of his own. Melvin was practicing his lawn tennis, batting the ball back and forth with Talos the footman. I was wearing my wings as usual, so if the ball flew off the ship I could retrieve it before it hit the waves.

"Aerostat ahoy!" Prissy called from the spar, where she was practicing her circus act.

Wally stepped back from the small pile of explosive powder he had been about to ignite and shoved up his goggles. He leaped onto the railing and shaded his eyes. Another vessel was advancing briskly toward us through the sky.

"Do you recognize her, Father?" he asked.

Oliver took a spyglass from his belt for a better look.

"No," he said. "But she certainly has a unique mode of locomotion!"

I settled on the rail beside Wally, squinting against the ocean's glare. Oliver's observation was correct. There were multiple paddles spinning on each side of the approaching aerostat's long hull. She resembled a centipede crawling through the air.

"Are they Mesmers?" Prissy asked.

"I don't think so," Calypso said. "Mesmers don't seem the type to use technology."

"They are probably just fellow travelers in the sky," Melvin said. "I say, they're moving along quite well. I wonder if they could be persuaded to give us a tow?"

"What provides her power?" Wally wondered.

"Old-fashioned velocipedes on deck, evidently," Oliver said, handing over the spyglass. "Their pedals power the paddles, apparently."

Everyone but Mr. Tesla, who was in the lab below, had gathered at the rail to watch the ship.

"Clever," Calypso approved. "I wonder who captains her?"

It was a question I felt would soon be answered, as she was approaching us at an alarming rate. I could see crewmen now, manning the velocipedes.

Oliver snatched up his bullhorn.

"Correct your course!" he called. "We are going to collide!"

The paddles stilled, and the captain of the strange aerostat spoke through a bullhorn of his own.

"Are you the Kennewicketts?"

"Yes," Oliver replied. "Do I know you, sir?"

A black flag sprang up—clearly by means of wires, as there was no wind—revealing the image of a skull over crossbones.

"Good gads." Melvin gasped. "They're not Mesmers. They're pirates!"

Melvin was correct. Even without a breeze, I could smell salty sweat and stale rum on the ruffians.

"We have no gold on board," Prissy said. "What could they possibly want?"

"Nikola's inventions," Calypso guessed. "They would be worth more than gold to some people."

The war of the currents! I had forgotten that Wally wasn't the only one in danger.

"Inform Nikola of our visitors, Walter," Calypso said quietly.

"Yes, Mother," Wally said.

"You might inquire when the receiver will be finished as well," Oliver added. "Suggest that sooner might be better than later."

"Surrend-*aargh!*" the pirate captain bellowed.

"Hurry, Walter. I will attempt to buy time," Calypso said, reaching for the bullhorn. "Do you mean 'surrender'?" she asked pleasantly. "Please enunciate more clearly."

"Surrend-er," the pirate said, with evident effort, "the Wizard of the West to us! We've been paid good money for that man's head. Give him up, if you wish this to end without bloodshed."

Wally stopped in his tracks, and I ran into his knees. *They didn't want Mr. Tesla's inventions. They were after his brain!* We had no time to listen further.

We hurried below deck and found the Wizard working on a very large black box.

"Pardon the interruption, sir," Wally began politely but with haste. Calypso believes that urgency is no excuse for ill manners. "We are under attack by pirates. My parents have sent me to inquire as to when the propulsion device for the *Daedalus* might be done. Father suggested sooner might be better than later."

"Did the pirates have any demands?" Mr. Tesla asked.

Wally looked uncomfortable. "They want your head, sir."

"Severed, or in place and functioning?"

"I'm afraid that wasn't clear."

"I see." Mr. Tesla nodded. "It could go either way in the current wars. Regardless, it will take two hours to have a functional device. I'm afraid it can't be done sooner. Stall them!"

"We'll do our best, then, sir," Wally said.

We returned to deck to find a terrifying tableau. The pirates were closer, and they positively bristled with blades.

"Do you intend to deliver the Wizard to us?" the pirate captain queried.

"Never, you scurvy dogs!" Calypso replied.

I felt it was unfair to compare them to dogs. That was being far too kind.

"Mr. Tesla would like us to resist for at least two hours," Wally told his parents.

"That's not good news." Oliver produced a sword from his walking stick.

"Board them, men!" the pirate bellowed. "Capture the young ones by force! You can toss the copper-topped kid to the sharks. I hear he causes trouble."

The blaggard meant Wally!

A "blaggard" is a person with a rotten heart. The kind of person I would never let near Walter Kennewickett! I bared my fangs and launched myself into the air, prepared to fight to the death.

11

N oodles!" Wally caught my tail and pulled me into his arms. "You wouldn't stand a chance against so many. There must be another way!"

A pirate swung a grappling hook above his head, and it sailed toward us through the air.

A "grappling hook" is a device with multiple iron claws. When attached to the end of a rope and thrown at a ship, it can catch a railing, allowing another ship to be pulled alongside so the pirates can jump aboard.

The hook in question would have done precisely that, had Melvin not intercepted its arc with his lawn-tennis racket. He has an excellent backhand.

"Well done, Mel!" Wally cheered.

More pirates were producing grappling hooks. Oliver whirled and slashed with his sword, severing the line of the first one that caught. Knives stepped to his assistance, blades flashing, and detached hooks were soon left lying about the *Daedalus*'s deck, only to be collected and tossed overboard by the industrious Dustketeers. It was obvious to all that the pirates would run out of ropes before the automatons ran out of energy.

The *Daedalus* would not be boarded today! Unfortunately, this fact was obvious to the pirates as well.

"To the pedals!" the buccaneer bellowed. "Ram them! We'll fish the ones we want from the water and leave the rest for the sharks!" His crew leaped to obey. The dozens of air paddles started churning as the pirates pedaled madly.

Calypso dashed to the helm and turned the nose of the *Daedalus* toward the sky, but our airship could not rise quickly enough to escape. The black ship jumped forward, smashing her bow into our propellers, then bouncing away.

"I have an idea, Father," Wally said, grabbing a faux mast with one hand as the airship rammed into us again. "If we deploy my man-lifting kite, it will act as a sail. It will, however, most likely damage the hull."

Gizmo calculated quickly. "The possibility of complete hull failure is thirty percent."

"An acceptable risk," Oliver said, "considering the alternative."

Wally raced to the rail cannon and pulled the covering off the kite. He settled his goggles in place, then grabbed the lever.

"Hang on!" he shouted as he pulled. The kite

shot skyward, the steel line unspooling behind it. I held my breath as it blossomed, spreading its massive wings among the altostratus clouds above us.

The line went taut, and several things happened almost instantaneously: the *Daedalus* leaped forward; the enormous initial force popped two of the bolts that held the steel reel to the ship; Jeeves caught Prissy as she slid across the deck; and Oliver, who had been assisting Knives, tumbled over the railing, catching the line he had been about to sever with one hand.

"Uncle!" Melvin cried, jumping to his aid.

Prissy assisted him and together they hauled Oliver back on board. The metal of the *Daedalus*'s skin groaned, and more bolts—from her joints, this time—*ping*ed into the air as we pulled away from the pirates.

The buccaneer called out commands to his crew, but they could pedal no faster.

"We will have to cut the kite's cable, Walter," Gizmo said as the pirates disappeared over the horizon. "The ship's structure can't take the strain."

Knives produced his best cable shears, and

the deed was done. Wally watched the kite float away as the *Daedalus* slowed and then hung in the air once more.

"Is everyone still on board?" Calypso queried.

"All accounted for, except—"

"Mr. Tesla!" Wally cried.

We raced below deck and found that the famous scientist had no more than a bump on his head from being thrown across the room. The doughty Dustketeers went to work setting the lab to rights.

"No need to apologize, Walter," Mr. Tesla said as Wally expressed his regrets while helping him to his feet. "Your quick thinking apparently saved us all. Especially me."

At that very moment, Gizmo stepped into the lab.

"We are slowly sinking," she announced.

This time, even Mr. Tesla raced to the deck.

Oliver checked his gauges. "We're at two thousand feet. The damaged hull must be leaking gas."

"This does complicate the rescue," Calypso

said. "And I doubt the pirates have given up. They seemed quite determined."

"May I suggest you repair the propellers?" Mr. Tesla asked. "I will finish the receiver."

Mr. Tesla's estimate of two hours was indeed correct. But it required yet another hour to see it installed.

It took Oliver and Calypso, both clipped onto safety lines, slightly longer to finish fixing the propellers. Wally remained on deck, ready to send down tools as requested. I flew between them, carrying what was needed.

Night was rising from the east, pushing the remains of the day out of the western sky, when Prissy spotted the pirates. The black ship was an undulating silhouette against the sunset.

"Finished!" Calypso called, and Jeeves pulled both her and Oliver back up over the railings.

The pirates were once again close enough for us to smell when Mr. Tesla pushed the button to turn the receiver on. An electric wind washed over me, and my hair stood on end.

Suddenly, the propellers were moving surprisingly fast. More surprising still was the ghostly green glow that bloomed from the tips of the faux masts, spars, and bowsprit.

"Saint Elmo's fire!" Melvin gasped.

"Radiant matter," Gizmo corrected. "Neither solid, liquid, nor gas. Hypothesized by Faraday in 1816; finally created in a laboratory by Sir William Crookes in 1879."

"Faraday was a brilliant man," Mr. Tesla said. "If you want to discover the secrets of the universe, think in terms of energy, frequency, and vibration!"

I'm sure there were multiple sightings of the *Flying Dutchman* that night as we fled eastward over the ocean, glowing eerily, the pirates lost behind us.

12

Waves were lapping at the *Daedalus* by the time we reached the Bay of Biscay. We were making a beeline for Bordeaux, the aerostat skipping like a stone across the water as its helium continued to leak out, causing it to sink ever lower.

"You may have to fly, Noodles," Wally said as he buttoned me into my winged vest. I licked his nose. That was nonsense, of course. If the ship sank, I would stay with Wally to the last.

Mr. Tesla and Oliver continued to inventory items that might be tossed overboard to lighten the ship. I had watched Gizmo's pots and pans, puddings and pastries go with great regret. We had subsisted for the past day on meager meals made from the few items that hadn't been discarded. But I understood the necessity. If the *Daedalus* sank beneath the waves, Mr. Tesla and the Kennewicketts might manage to swim or float, but the salt water would wreak havoc on the automatons.

"Land ho!" Calypso cried, pointing ahead.

"Pirates ho," Jeeves replied, pointing at the sky centipede that had appeared behind us.

I darted across the deck and flung myself into the air, wagging wildly to stay above the water, circling up and over the wounded *Daedalus*. The pesky pirates were indeed hot on our trail, paddles churning as they came. They must have pedaled all night. In the opposite direction I could make out a long stretch of sand, and trees beyond.

"Gizmo!" Oliver called below me. "Speed and distance calculations?"

Gizmo jumped on the rail, studying first the shoreline and then the fast-approaching pirate ship.

"We will make it to shore, sir," the automaton said as I alighted beside her.

"But what then?" Melvin asked.

"One conundrum at a time, dear," Calypso said. "Prepare to disembark."

Not many belongings were left for us to take along. Most personal items had been tossed overboard. Wally gathered the anti-Mesmer headgear while Gizmo rounded up the Dustketeers and tucked them in her pockets.

Time seemed to telescope as the damaged *Daedalus* hopped toward land, the pirates drawing ever closer.

Gizmo had calculated correctly. We reached the shore while the black ship was still some distance away—but not so far that I couldn't see people on its deck.

Oliver and Mr. Tesla jumped out when our ship scraped bottom, and pulled the *Daedalus* well up onto the beach before anyone else exited.

Jeeves shouldered the trunk containing our remaining possessions, and everyone abandoned ship. I landed in the deep sand beside Wally and ran beside him toward the tree line. I had just turned back to gauge the pirates' progress when Prissy screamed.

I whirled to find myself face-to-face with a nightmare.

An enormous spider was stepping over the trees. Its shovel-like palpi were waving wildly, and its massive maw, dripping some disgusting fluid, snapped open and shut.

"That's not good," Oliver said.

I had to agree.

The creature's eight enormous eyes flashed red and yellow as it leaned toward us.

I felt like a fly fixed in the monster's gaze.

"Bonjour," it boomed cheerfully. "Do you require assistance?"

"Yes, please, Monsieur Fevre!" shouted Wally. Until that moment my mind had been too muddled to realize I was looking at the *Arachne*.

The land yacht's long legs bent in multiple places, until her belly rested on the ground. A door opened to reveal an amiable young man in a velvet smoking jacket and an admirable brown

ascot. I tried not to gasp at the sight of him. Monsieur Fevre had no need of trousers or boots. I had seen guests at the Automated Inn conveyed by means of wheeled chairs, but this was something different altogether. Our rescuer's lower body was encased in a miniature version of the *Arachne*.

Calypso caught Prissy as she fainted.

"Forgive me!" Monsieur Fevre cried, taking an uncertain step backwards, a horrified look on his face. "I had no intention of shocking anyone, I assure you."

He looked at Wally, then at me. "You are the Kennewicketts, yes? Walter Kennewickett, with Noodles? But you must be! I had assumed you would have all been aware"—he waved at his mechanical, many-legged chair—"of this!"

"I never thought to mention it," Wally said, turning pink. "It didn't seem important." He stepped forward and offered his hand. "I'm very glad to meet you, sir!"

"It is you who must forgive us," Calypso

said, fanning Prissy, who was coming around. "Prissy's had a very tiring day already."

Prissy managed to stay on her feet while introductions were made.

"The Wizard of the West!" Monsieur Fevre inclined his head toward Mr. Tesla. "I am honored!"

"I have heard many good things about your inventions, sir," the Wizard replied.

"I say," Melvin shook the gentleman's hand, "you and your machine are terrifically timely!"

"Not so terrifically." Monsieur Fevre shrugged. "I received a mysterious message from your president. It was full of phrases such as 'lend assistance' and 'life or death'! I calculated your probable path, and I have patrolled the beaches up and down for days now."

"We certainly appreciate it," Oliver said. "Are you aware that the *Arachne* is leaking hydraulic fluid?"

"Hydraulics" is a branch of science concerned with the conveyance of pressurized liquids through pipes to produce mechanical movement.

"Non!" Monsieur Fevre cried, scurrying out on the sand to look up at the still-waving palpi and dripping maw. "Not again! This is troublesome, but not serious, I assure you. The difficulty is in making a system of this size. The pressure must be immense."

Apparently malfunctions plague inventors everywhere.

"I'd love to take a look." Oliver produced a pipe-bender from his pocket.

"Oliver is always prepared to render assistance," confided Calypso. "And *I* am always interested in mechanical methods of locomotion."

"I might have an idea or two as well," Mr. Tesla suggested.

"If you will pardon me, madams and sirs," Jeeves said, "might I point out that the pirates are fast approaching?"

We turned to find that the centipede ship was almost ashore.

139

"They are after you?" Monsieur Fevre asked.

"Technically, they wish to acquire Mr. Tesla's head," Oliver clarified.

"We are not sure if their contract requires his body as well," Calypso added, "and if so, in what condition."

"Mon Dieu!" the Frenchman cried. "But this will not do. Alphonse!" he called. "Our guests will board immediately!"

We were assisted aboard by crewmen dressed uniformly in black pants and striped shirts, with kerchiefs around their necks. Each had one arm adorned with an excellent spider tattoo.

"Never fear, Kennewicketts!" Monsieur Fevre declared once we were all safely inside the contraption's pseudo-cephalothorax. He settled onto a podium, which apparently served as the captain's seat. The land yacht rose smoothly to stand at full height. "The *Arachne* is faster than any airship!"

I felt as if I were sitting in a treehouse. Without the tree, of course.

"When last we corresponded," Wally said, "you had achieved a speed of sixty miles per hour!"

Monsieur Fevre's hand flew to his heart. "Walter, you wound me! *Arachne* runs seventy-two *miles per hour*, as you Americans say—more than one hundred fifteen kilometers per hour, by European measurements—if the ground is level. That is faster than any locomotive, yes? You will see! Where do we go?"

"Peschiera, Italy," Calypso replied. "On Lake Garda."

"Over the Alps, then! That will make her a little slower."

"The Alps" is a mighty mountain range that runs between France and Italy.

"Not to worry. We shall have you there by morning."

141

The *Arachne* started to move. It was as if the treehouse were lightly tossed by the wind.

When we were safely underway, Monsieur Fevre turned the bridge over to his captain and kindly offered us multiple tour options. Melvin and Prissy opted to explore the luxurious lounge, as Prissy craved a calming cup of tea. Calypso, Oliver, Wally, and Mr. Tesla headed for the engine rooms to examine the hydraulic system.

I followed Knives, Gizmo, and the other automatons to the galley at the invitation of a captivating chef, who seemed quite taken by Gizmo's grasp of various ingredients.

"A doggie!" the kitchen maid cried in delight as we entered. I had always found French visitors at the Automated Inn to be quite fond of canine companions.

I spent the afternoon in the galley nibbling escargot, caviar on crackers, and petit fours. I much preferred it to looking out the window. Every time I ventured a glance outside, I found that something terrible was happening: we were scaling sheer cliffs in chilling shortcuts between

railroad lines, or tiptoeing over trestles at terrific speeds. Luckily, the cabin was cleverly sus-
pended so that it stayed level no matter what the
Arachne was doing.

"But won't your hydraulics cease to work
in the mountains?" Wally was asking when we
gathered again in the control room. "The cold
will congeal the oil."

"Not at all!" Monsieur Fevre replied. "The
oil is warmed by the coal furnace. But we will
not be crawling over the mountains. There is no
railroad where we must go. We will fly!"

The *Arachne* had climbed to the top of a lone spire of rock. Everyone rushed to the windows.

Working levers and cables himself, Monsieur Fevre balanced her like a top upon the stone. I felt only a slight shift as the abdomen rose above the pseudo-cephalothorax and emitted an enormous hot-air balloon.

As soon as we were airborne, everyone retired to the dining hall. We feasted on *flamiche*, which turned out to be a lovely cheese pie, as the mountains of the Alps passed like rows of ragged fangs beneath us, icy in the moonlight.

I finally found myself curled up by Wally in the charming guest room, but I couldn't sleep. We'd left the pirates behind, but tomorrow we would face the Mesmers.

13

Do you receive this welcome wherever you go?" Oliver asked, obviously envious of the stir the *Arachne* caused when we arrived on the outskirts of Peschiera. The eight-legged wonder generated more commotion than even the *Daedalus* had the day she'd hovered over the ice cream shop in Gasket Gully.

"I've grown used to it." Monsieur Fevre sighed. "Arachnids are so misunderstood! I'll prepare my crew to assist you in apprehending the villainous Mesmers."

"I wish they could"—Calypso settled her stylish hat in place and checked the goggles—"but it would be unwise."

"We have protective headgear for only six people, sir," Wally explained.

"You mean my crew would be at the Mesmers' mercy?" Monsieur Fevre asked as Wally adjusted a special modification Calypso had made to his aforementioned gear. She had created a mask to keep him from being affected by feathers.

"They have no mercy," Melvin declared, helping Prissy adjust her hat. "They have ordered those under their control to do unspeakable things."

"Such as plunging from precipices," Prissy said with a shudder. "We must find Mother and Father, Mel! I can't stand the thought of them under the Mesmers' power!"

"This is it," Oliver said, picking up his sword cane. "It's time to save the world!"

I would have wagged if I hadn't been wearing my wings. Madini would soon be put away where he could never menace Wally again.

"Did you notice the number of pigeons in the air when we arrived?" Mr. Tesla asked after we'd bid Monsieur Fevre farewell and stepped onto the street.

I had. And I had known as soon as the

Arachne's door opened that we had discovered the coop of the peculiar Columbidae. *Peschiera reeked of popcorn. And popcorn was Iron Claw's favorite food.*

"Keep in mind," Oliver said, "that it is not just Mesmers we must worry about. Anyone we meet might be under their power. We must do our best to detain Madini without harming the citizenry. Once we have the Mesmer mastermind, the war will be won!"

Walter led the way down the narrow street, and I went with him. Oliver and Calypso were close behind. The automatons followed.

We came around a corner, and Wally stopped. The couple who stood before us could only be Wentworth and Mame Kennewickett. Wentworth looked rather like Oliver, but with less hair. Mame was very like Prissy, only with more fluff around the middle. Both were impeccably dressed, as befitted the pater- and materfamilias of such an illustrious clan.

"Mother!" Prissy cried, rushing forward to embrace the woman.

"Prissy, darling," Mame said, giving her a peck on the cheek, "how good to see you, and what an odd hat."

"Melvin." Wentworth shook his son's hand. "You've grown exceptionally large."

Wally and I exchanged a look. Wentworth and Mame were not the least bit surprised to see us. This clearly bothered Melvin as well.

"Have you met a man called Madini recently, Father?" Melvin asked.

"Can't say that I have. How are you, Oliver?" he asked, turning toward his brother. "I say, you've brought an army of automatons with you, as well as your wife, your son, and his dog. And could this be Nikola Tesla?"

Oliver introduced the Wizard of the West.

"Who's minding the Inn?" Wentworth asked when the introductions were over.

"We left it in excellent hands," Oliver assured him. "If you haven't met Madini, do you know a Signore Giuseppe?"

"Why, of course we know him," Mame said. "He's the mayor!"

"Pride of his people," Wentworth went on. "King of the coop. Why don't you take off your hats and stay awhile? We'll hop right over to see him!"

"Hop?" Melvin asked, looking at him askance.

"Strut. I mean, stroll! Let's stroll right over! Lovely day for a stroll." He tilted his head and watched a bug scurry across the walk.

"Mother," Prissy said, "are you both . . . quite well?"

"Of course, dear," the materfamilias said. "We're both in fine feather. Er, fettle. Come and meet the mayor."

By "fine fettle," she meant they were in an excellent state of fitness and form. I could tell that not even Prissy believed that.

"Of course we will," Calypso agreed, giving Wally and the others a significant look. "Lead on!"

Wally stepped aside and let them show the way.

"Be alert," I overheard Gizmo instruct the automatons quietly. She caught a Dustketeer as it tried to drop from her pocket, and tucked it away again. "We are in the Mesmers' lair."

Mr. Tesla studied the pigeons that lined the rooftops and followed our progress with their beady black eyes.

"They don't seem as friendly as usual," he said.

I couldn't say. Pigeons had never seemed friendly to me.

My hackles stood on end long before we reached the town square. The people of Peschiera seemed to be going about their business, but there was no smell of fish or garlic from the food stands. Not even from the fishermen mending their nets. The *whole town* smelled of popcorn.

"Ah! There he is!" Wentworth pointed. "Signore Giuseppe himself." We all turned to see a mustachioed man sitting at a street café. It was Madini, of course.

The king of the coop removed the lid from a tureen on the table. It should have been full of something delicious, such as *acqua pazza*, a fine fish soup. It was filled instead with puffy white corn. He tossed a piece to Mame, who pecked it out of the air.

"What do you think, Walter?" the Mesmer asked, glancing up at our group. "Could you tell they were mesmerized? We're getting better, yes?"

"Your techniques have improved," Wally agreed. "I could hardly tell."

A shadow swept over our heads.

Iron Claw. The feathered fiend alighted atop a light pole.

"You're trying to trick us again, Walter." The pigeon and Madini spoke in unison.

I had forgotten how horrible the effect was.

Oliver stepped toward the Mesmer, but at that moment the man rose, spreading his arms like wings.

"Now, my minions!" the blended voices of the man and pigeon cried.

I lunged for Madini's leg, but Wentworth caught me by the tail and held me aloft. People began pouring out of the shops around us.

Oliver, Calypso, and Wally had once fought

off a roomful of mesmerized popcorn vendors. However, I was not sure even the mighty Kennewicketts could stand up to an entire town.

Two of the fishermen leaped upon Knives and ripped his bladed hands from his wrists. Jeeves grabbed the scoundrels and knocked their heads together.

"Capture them!" Madini cried.

Wentworth flung me at the automatons, and I landed on Jeeves just in time to become entangled in a fishnet cast over everyone who had rushed to Knives's aid—in other words, all the automatons. We floundered furiously until the net was drawn so tightly that none of us could move. Meanwhile, Wally, Oliver, and Calypso had assumed their best judo positions, Melvin and Mr. Tesla prepared for fisticuffs, and even Prissy held her parasol like a weapon.

But there were too many townspeople under the Mesmers' control. The automatons fought to free themselves from the net, but to no avail. We could only watch as, one by one, the Kennewick-etts were overcome by the crowd and had their Mesmer-proof headgear snatched away. One by one, they fell under the spell of Iron Claw's spinning eye and went still. All but Wally.

"Not him," Madini said as a minion reached for Wally's mask. "I prefer to make him suffer." He turned to address Wally. "I've spent many hours examining your room, Walter. Do you realize that you sometimes leave your journal there? I've read it. *I know your fears.*"

"I'm not afraid of you," the brave boy said.

"You should be," Madini replied. "But you are afraid of yourself instead. You're afraid because you know you are so very much like Mad Mars. Need I mention your bizarre belief that Iron Claw is the mastermind of the Mesmers?"

The pigeon on the lamppost spread its wings, and Madini laughed.

153

"Mad Mars was prone to peculiar theories, wasn't he, Walter? I spent many hours in his study as well as in your room. Reading your journal was just like reading his notes. The same fixation with flight. The same attention to detail. Shall I pinpoint the moment Mars started to go mad? It was the moment when no one in his family believed his bizarre theories anymore. *What kind of Kennewickett are you, Walter?*"

Wally swallowed. I could tell he was shaken.

"You are not mad, Walter!" Gizmo called.

"You are the exceedingly good sort of Kennewickett, young sir," Jeeves agreed.

"Take these machines to the foundry," Iron Claw screeched, "and dispose of them!"

That did not sound pleasant. A "foundry" is an establishment in which molten metal is poured into molds. We found ourselves being dragged up the street by a horde of mesmerized fishermen.

I craned my neck, trying to get one last look at Wally. And then I noticed Knives's hand was following us along the road, razorlike fingertips tapping on the cobbles as it came. For an instant I thought that Calypso had made yet another modification—and then I heard the tiny, tinny battle song of the Dustketeers.

All was not lost!

The courageous clockwork cleaners had slipped from Gizmo's pocket and appropriated the bladed appendage! They reached the back of the mob and began dodging booted feet, making their way ever closer.

I whined encouragement. They made it past the crowd and managed a single *shnick* of a fin-

gertip through the net before their rescue attempt was delayed by a pair of size-nine fishing boots.

I shoved my head out through the hole, but my wings stuck.

"Noodles!" Wally's voice echoed down the stone street. "I need you!"

With one mighty squirm, I was through the netting. *Dachshunds do not abandon their best friends.*

I dashed past the Dust Bunnies, who had collected Knives's hand and were chasing after the automatons once more, and raced down the road.

Wally was sitting on the street, and Iron Claw was still perched atop the lamppost, bobbing his hideous head. Mr. Tesla and the Kennewicketts were pecking about with the pigeons on the sidewalk, oblivious to what was happening.

"You've gone mad," Madini cooed at Wally. "Just like Mars." He hadn't seen me yet.

I had one chance. If Madini was the mastermind, I could distract him long enough to break his power over the Kennewicketts. But if Iron Claw was the one in control, attacking Madini would do nothing.

I raced across the square and launched myself into the sky. Walter Kennewickett believed Iron Claw was the mastermind.

The pigeon lifted from the lamppost in alarm. Suddenly, the air around me was full of wings, beaks, and talons as more birds rose. I exploded through them like a skyrocket, my eyes fixed on a single evil fowl.

Iron Claw folded his wings and dived, trying to escape me among the twisting streets.

I had chased too many Dust Bunnies not to anticipate this move. We winged through the narrow alleyways and dodged awnings and signs. I saw the Dustketeers catch up to the netted automatons once more as we streaked overhead, and it distracted me for one disastrous moment.

Iron Claw turned, talons extended. They caught me as I passed, ripping my ear, but I wheeled, and the chase was on again. The pigeon was a master of the air, folding his wings to fit through bell towers, climbing into the sun. But wherever he went, I followed two flaps behind.

As we crossed the square once more, I risked another glance below and saw that the automatons had escaped the nets and were rushing to the Kennewicketts' aid.

We were directly above them when I managed to get close enough to Iron Claw to snap my jaws. Apparently all twelve alien rectrices are fully detachable.

The peculiar pigeon uttered a terrible cry as he fell from the sky. *Tail failure may cause tragedy.*

Jeeves, thinking fast, caught the tumbling bird in Madini's soup tureen and popped the lid on tight, hiding that horrible pinwheel eye.

Bakers, fishmongers, businessmen, and even Madini, blinked in confusion. The shock of losing his tail array had apparently broken the evil bird's control over his minions.

"What happened?" Calypso asked, hand to her head.

"Justice has been served, madam," Jeeves said, offering her the dish.

"Noodles!" Wally cried, scooping me up. "You believed me!"

Of course I did.

Walter Kennewickett is the smartest boy in the world.

EPILOGUE

We went on to visit the contessa, who kindly arranged for the capture of the pirates who were so persistently pursuing Mr. Tesla. The captain was imprisoned, but the crew was offered clemency. Several of the less hardened pirates accepted and went on to form an unstoppable bicycle-racing team. The Wizard of

the West said his goodbyes and went to visit his family.

Melvin, Prissy, and their prodigal parents accepted an invitation from Monsieur Fevre to tour Europe aboard the *Arachne*. Oliver, Calypso, and Wally were invited too, but couldn't bear to be away from their labs any longer. The automatons were anxious to get home as well, especially Gizmo. She had collected many excellent recipes in Italy and was eager to share them with Mr. Jones.

When we arrived in Gasket Gully, everyone threw confetti to welcome us home ... Except Mrs. McDivit, who threw rocks.

Apparently not even saving the world is good enough for some people.

AUTHOR'S NOTE

Nikola Tesla, the "Wizard of the West" who helps the Kennewicketts in this story, was real, though his adventures and some of the inventions in this book are fictional. The "war of the currents" was real too, and Tesla did discover the alternating current that we all use in our homes today.

Tesla was a brilliant Serbian American scientist and electrical engineer. He was also a very peculiar person, with a passion for feeding pigeons in the park. Although he was horrified by war, he tried to market a death ray, and he claimed to have built an earthquake machine.

Tesla *did* discover x-rays, and he invented electric generators, radio, electric motors, radio-controlled vehicles, and much, much more. In fact, he held more than two hundred and fifty patents, and many more of his inventions were never patented at all.

Some of his most spectacular experiments were conducted at his laboratory in Colorado Springs, where he built an artificial lightning tower. Arcs of blue electricity climbed a giant coil, scenting the air with ozone as bolts 135 feet long crackled from a mast atop the tower. Thunder from the man-made lightning could be heard as far as fifteen miles away.

Some people say light bulbs would glow if you carried them within 100 feet of the tower, even with no wires attached; horses nearby bolted when electricity arced from the ground to their iron shoes; even butterflies that flew around the tower were electrified, swirling in circles with halos of Saint Elmo's fire on their wings.

There have been many other astounding stories about Tesla and his inventions, but scientists have been unable to verify some of the stranger claims. Tesla's documentation and equipment were lost in a series of lab fires, allowing myth and misinformation to work its way into the mystery surrounding the great man.

Some of the things Tesla is said to have done are (or seem to be) scientifically impossible. But no one can deny that Nikola Tesla had an amazing scientific mind, or that his actual inventions changed the world!

If you'd like to know more about the science and history in *The Ire of Iron Claw*, or want to exercise your imagination, ramp up your research, and polish your problem-solving skills, download the educator's guide created by Debbie Gonzales and designed by Moriah Ellig at www.hmhco.com/shop/books/The-Ire-of-Iron-Claw/9780544225022.

About the Author
and Illustrator

KERSTEN HAMILTON is the author of several picture books and many novels, including the critically acclaimed young adult trilogy the Goblin Wars. She has worked as a ranch hand, a wood-cutter, a lumberjack, a census taker, a wrangler for wilderness guides and an archeological surveyor. Now, when she's not writing, she hunts dinosaurs in the deserts and badlands of New Mexico and tends to the animals on her farm in Kentucky. For more about Kersten, please visit www.kerstenhamilton.com.

JAMES HAMILTON is an artist and designer who lives in San Matco, California. This is his second book.

DON'T MISS BOOK 3 IN
THE GADGETS AND GEARS SERIES:

WALLY AND NOODLES are back to the business of
scientific innovation—and fun. In London, they meet a
young pickpocket named Dobbin who works for a mysterious criminal called the Tick-Tock Man. Soon they are
racing through secret tunnels in a bid to help Dobbin's little sister. Can the brave boy-scientist and his loyal sidekick
find the one person who can save her before it's too late?

Turn the page for a sneak peek at
The Tick-Tock Man!

1

Tick-tock.

The sound was unsettling, and when you are with a Kennewickett, anything unsettling could spell disaster.

My name is Noodles. It is my duty to keep Walter Kennewickett, boy genius and scientist in training, as far from disasters as possible. It is my privilege as his best friend to accompany him everywhere he goes.

Which is why I found myself on a dark street corner in London, trying to track the source of the mysterious sound.

London was aglow with the process of electrification and hummed with activity even at night. Cable cars mixed with horse-drawn cabs and carts, and many of the thousand lamps that lit the streets had been converted from gas to electricity.

But Wally wasn't interested in well-lit streets. The dim gaslight above was perfect for his purposes.

Tick-tock.

I could sense approaching danger, but I could not tell from which direction it would arrive. The sound was bouncing off bricks, glass, and cobblestones.

"What was that, Noodles?" Wally asked, lowering the handheld camera he had been adjusting.

Walter Kennewickett is a very observant boy.

"Probably a rat," his aunt Rhodope said. "London crawls with them after dark."

Miss Rhodope Pickering is the youngest of Calypso Kennewickett's sisters. The fact that Rhodope is an eccentric allows her to fly kites in the park while other people her age attend university.

The fact that she is a sought-after photographic artist allows her to keep comfortable rooms in Charing Cross. The Pickerings are an artistic family. My current conundrum was the result of Wally's mother, Calypso, mentioning that he might have inherited an aptitude for art.

An "aptitude" is the natural ability to master a skill.

There were certainly many aptitudes Wally had inherited from his prodigious parents. His attempts at art, however, were dismal—until his father, Oliver, pointed out that the correct term for fireworks is "pyrotechnics," which means "art made from fire."

Generations of Kennewicketts have excelled at blowing things up. Wally is currently creating a line of pyrotechnics you might carry in your pocket and enjoy on any street corner.

Before we traveled to London to participate in the Electromobile Road Rally, Miss Rhodope had written to him, requesting that he use his experience with explosives to create a faster flash powder for use in photography. She'd promised to arrange a breakfast with her friend Sir Arthur Conan Doyle if he did. Walter Kennewickett is a fan of Sir Arthur's books and enjoys matching wits with his fictional detective Sherlock Holmes.

Wally had not only produced the powder for his aunt, but devised a hat to hold the flash device, and a trigger cable to attach his hand-held camera to it. We were preparing to photograph the participants in the Electromobile Rally, which would be coming down the road at any minute, followed by a small parade of Calypso Kennewickett's fans. Calypso was the only woman among the twelve participants in the three-country rally, which was a contest of speed, design, and dependability. Since Oliver and Calypso had worked together on every aspect of their elegant electrical carriage, the Zephyr, they were taking turns driving.

The Kennewicketts had won the first leg of the rally handily, arriving at Trafalgar Square two days ago and greeted by cheering crowds. The electromobile in last place had not arrived until just after sunset today.

The crowds had cheerfully gathered again. Drivers had signed autographs and posed for pictures for the press. Now they were proceeding to the docks at the Embankment, where ships had been chartered to carry them across the channel. The second leg of the rally was to be in France.

The Kennewicketts had requested that this small street be kept free of crowds to allow Rhodope to test her new technique for photographing in the dark. When Kennewickcttts ask a small favor, people tend to cooperate. They are world-famous scientists, after all.

"Attachment test," Wally said. "In three, two, one—"

The camera clicked and fire flashed, and someone uttered a terrible cry. I whirled as a tatterdemalion tumbled out of a dark doorway. A "tatterdemalion" is a person dressed in rags and tatters.

This old man's frock coat was so faded, it appeared gray in the lamplight, in contrast with his shock of wild white hair. His angular form and antique attire gave the impression that he had just fallen out of the pages of a novel by

Mr. Charles Dickens. The poor creature held his hands before his face, as if he were afraid of more flashes. He must have been looking directly at Wally when the powerful powder ignited.

He stumbled, and Wally leapt to his assistance. As Rhodope and I followed Wally across the street, I realized that we had discovered the source of the unsettling sound. The man himself was ticking.

"I'm so sorry, sir," Wally said, helping him toward a low windowsill where he could sit. "If I had known you were near, I would have called out a warning!"

"You've blinded me!" the stranger said in a strangled voice.

"It will pass presently," Rhodope reassured him. "And I'll summon a cab to carry you home."

"No, no, just let me sit," he said, still rubbing his eyes. "I'll fumble my way. It ain't far."

"I'll lead you there myself, sir," Wally offered. "If you'd only wait until the rally has passed!"

I shook my ears, thinking my instincts must have gone awry, but no—the ticking was definitely coming from the feeble old man. At any rate, it was soon drowned out by the approaching parade.

"They're coming!" Rhodope cried. "We'll have to photograph them from this side of the street. Get ready, Walter!" Wally quickly reloaded the flash powder.

The first vehicle to appear was a torpedo-shaped affair driven by Camille Jenatzy, nicknamed Le Diable Rouge, "the red devil," because of his unruly red beard. I felt a comparison to an annoyed Airedale might be more befitting.

Click-flash!

Jenatzy did not look pleased to have his photograph taken. He had set a speed record of sixty-two miles per hour in a similarly shaped electric automobile just four years ago. Last year, his record had fallen to a carriage with an internal combustion engine. Word was, Jenatzy had intended to take the record back on the England leg, but the Kennewicketts captured it instead.

Rhodope poured a measured amount of

powder into the contraption on Wally's head after each photograph was taken, then stepped back and shaded her eyes from the flash.

The Kennewicketts were twelfth in line.

Rhodope raised her own camera, and Wally detached his flash. The Zephyr had no batteries or Voltage Vats. It was powered by Nikola Tesla's recent invention that drew electric power directly from the aether, a mysterious medium he believes to exist in the spaces between the solid matter of the universe. I had listened attentively

to his explanations, but I still could not quite comprehend the concept or the contraption. An unexpected consequence of this type of power was the generation of radiant matter, better known as Saint Elmo's fire.

Cold blue flames played over the Zephyr's frame. Moths drawn to the light flitted through the energy field, and their wings lit with radiant matter, which didn't harm them in the least. They spun like frenzied fairies around the fantastic machine. It completely spoiled the effect. I felt that people who viewed the photos should be admiring the Kennewicketts, not some bedazzling bugs.

The Kennewicketts had requested the last place in line to allow Rhodope time to capture the phenomenon on film. Gizmo, the family's mechanical assistant, had asked for a photograph to share with the other automatons who had stayed home with her to staff the Kennewicketts' Automated Inn. They were now all powered by the same device that caused the Zephyr to glow, and free from Voltage Vats and charging stations forever. Fortunately, the effect that lit the Zephyr seemed to apply only when very large amounts of energy were drawn from the aether. Radiant automatons would no doubt have unsettled some of the Inn's guests.

"Ascot, Walter!" Calypso called as the Zephyr rolled to a stop.

I growled as one particularly persistent moth fluttered in front of the camera.

"Yes, Mother." Wally straightened his tie as he stepped forward. Walter Kennewickett is always impeccably dressed. Calypso feels that a tidy appearance is a sign of a tidy mind.

I kept my eyes on the moths. I was quite sure Calypso would not approve of an insect obscuring Walter's face in the family photo.

Wally turned to pose by the Zephyr's door. At that moment a moth made the mistake of flitting toward the fender. I leapt, and snapped my jaws about it. I did not swallow it, of course. Well-bred dachshunds do not ingest insects.

"Nicely done, Noodles," Oliver said, surrep-

titiously checking his own tie before smiling for
the camera.

"No manufacture of pyrotechnics while we
are gone, son," he went on, turning to Wally.
"Listen to your aunt Rhodope."

"Certainly, Father."

The wiggling inside my mouth was becoming unbearable. I tried to distract myself by spinning in place.

Finally, Rhodope lowered her camera and I
heard Calypso shift the Zephyr into gear.

"Spit it out, Noodles," she said. "And take care of Walter for us."

I ejected the insect onto the pavement and attempted to regain my dignity as it crawled away.

"Get a picture of the Union with the flash, Walter!" Rhodope cried as the Zephyr rolled on. She meant the members of the International Union of Women's Suffrage Societies who were marching behind the Zephyr.

"Suffrage" is the right to vote in political elections. Calypso was a founding member of the organization. She felt that it was ridiculous that women who were doctors, journalists, artists, or inventors extraordinaire could not cast a ballot. Fire flashed, and the Sisters of Suffrage—with their shoulder sashes that read "Equal Rights for Women!" and their "Calypso Kennewickett" banners—were captured on film.

Rhodope cheered as the Sisters passed, followed by two constables who appeared to be keeping an eye on them.

A "constable" is a British police officer.

"Come on, Walter," Rhodope said. "Let's see our new friend home."

Wally turned to retrieve the tattered man, but the fellow was nowhere to be found.

"The dazzle must have worn off," Rhodope said. "He's found his own way. Let's follow the parade instead!"